'That's the first time you've ever said my name.' His voice was harsh and deep and textured with hunger. 'Paige.'

Only one syllable, yet it was a caress, a note of raw need, a sensual promise.

But he waited, his eyes keen and measuring as they raked her face.

What was he doing? Demanding that she take the first step to surrender?

A stray raindrop plopped onto her lips, startling her into licking it off. He made a soft, feral sound that sent chills scudding the length of her spine, and the next moment she was being strained against his big, aroused body and he was kissing her, his mouth cool and controlled against hers—for a mini-second.

Until his steely discipline shattered into splinters and they kissed like long-separated lovers, as though they had kissed a thousand times before—as though after this there would be no other kiss, no other touch

Robyn Donald has always lived in Northland in New Zealand, initially on her father's stud dairy farm at Warkworth, then in the Bay of Islands, an area of great natural beauty, where she lives today with her husband and an ebullient and mostly Labrador dog. She resigned her teaching position when she found she enjoyed writing romances more, and now spends any time not writing in reading, gardening, travelling and writing letters to keep up with her two adult children and her friends.

THE MILLIONAIRE'S VIRGIN MISTRESS

BY
ROBYN DONALD

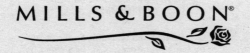

All the characters in this book have no existence outside the imagination of the author, and have no relation whatsoever to anyone bearing the same name or names. They are not even distantly inspired by any individual known or unknown to the author, and all the incidents are pure invention.

First published in Great Britain 2003
Harlequin Mills & Boon Limited,
Eton House, 18-24 Paradise Road, Richmond, Surrey TW9 1SR

© Robyn Donald 2003

ISBN 0 263 83333 X

Set in Times Roman 10½ on 12 pt.
01-1103-48533

Printed and bound in Spain
by Litografía Rosés, S.A., Barcelona

CHAPTER ONE

'MARK, do you think she's one of the strippers? Or...' a significant pause followed by a little laugh '...do they parade her now and then as a horrible example of what can happen if you aren't careful?'

Heat stung Paige Howard's skin, although she acquitted the speaker of deliberate rudeness; the woman couldn't know that a trick of acoustics carried every cut-glass syllable from the foyer of the old hotel to the top of the staircase.

And the posters for the club on the upper floor, offering lap dancing and massage, were too blatant to miss. It was an understandable mistake to assume that Paige was one of the women who offered their services to any man with the money to pay for them.

However, she wasn't going to tell them that she'd never seen the inside of the strip bar! She had more important things to worry about than a momentary humiliation. Frowning, she glanced at the baby in her arms, worried by his increasingly flushed little face.

The woman and her Mark would be tourists on one of the routes that showed off Napier's stunning collection of Art Deco buildings, built after a devastating earthquake seventy years previously. The small city on the sweep of New Zealand's Hawke Bay was now a destination for pilgrims who enjoyed both the architecture and the superb wines of the region.

Paige knew she'd never see this couple again, and she didn't care a five-dollar note what they thought of her.

Although five dollars, she thought grimly, would come in handy right now. She had been made redundant a few weeks previously, and her meagre savings had almost disappeared.

When baby Brodie's temperature had got to the worrying stage she'd had to break the strip club's rules and contact his mother, who worked there. Sherry had thrust money for the doctor into her hands, and gone back to dancing with tears in her eyes.

Brows pinching together, Paige smoothed the shawl back from Brodie's crumpled little face, checking it with real fear building beneath her ribs. Dusky patches darkened the skin around his eyes and he was panting between pale, dry lips.

How could a baby—perfectly normal an hour ago—deteriorate so quickly?

At that moment he jerked in her arms, his face screwing up in pain although he made no noise. Increasing her speed as fast as she dared down the stairs, she pitched her voice to a low soothing murmur.

'Hush, darling. Shh, little man, we're on our way to the doctor and you'll soon feel much, much better…'

She'd almost reached the bottom of the staircase when the couple turned from their admiration of the panelled reception area. Unwillingly she glanced up. Her astounded gaze clashed with brilliant blue eyes in a dark, arrogantly aristocratic face—eyes that blazed with incredulous disbelief across the distance between them.

Not Mark, she thought sickly. *Marc.*

Marc Corbett.

'Paige!'

Irrational panic kicking her in the stomach, she missed the last step and pitched forwards. Hampered by the child in her arms, she instinctively twisted to protect him from the marble floor.

Cruelly strong hands bit into her waist, hauling her up against a lean, hard body, supporting her until she could gasp, 'I'm all right!'

Brodie's high-pitched wail cut through Marc Corbett's reply, but she could hear his deep voice reverberate through his chest, and for a moment—a brief, shocked second—she remembered what it had been like to be held in those arms as music swirled around them on the dance floor...

He let her go and demanded harshly, 'What the hell are you doing here?'

Brodie stiffened and shrieked again, the sound abruptly cutting off as though someone had clamped a hand across his mouth. His little body jerked, arms and legs thrashing wildly.

'What's the matter with that child?' Marc's voice cracked liked a whip.

Terror squeezing her heart, Paige scanned Brodie's unconscious face; his eyes were closed and his lips had turned an ominous purple.

'Oh, God, he's so sick,' she whispered, touching his forehead. The fine, soft skin burned the back of her hand. Terrified, she tightened her arms around him and swivelled, heading as fast as she could for the doors.

The woman with Marc said on a concerned note, 'I think it's having a convulsion.'

'Where's the nearest doctor?' Marc gripped Paige by the elbow, ignoring her mute resistance as he steered her up the street. 'Get into the car.'

He indicated a large BMW a few metres along the pavement, as timelessly elegant as the surrounding buildings. Paige bolted into the front passenger seat and gabbled directions at Marc, barely registering the woman who climbed into the back.

Marc glanced once over his shoulder before forcing his way into the stream of traffic, judging the narrow gap to a nicety. Heart hammering, Paige felt Brodie's small body relax. Oh, God, she thought feverishly, please, no. *Please*, no!

Almost sagging with relief, she saw his eyelids twitch; seconds later his lips gained a little healthy colour. He blinked a couple of times before giving a pathetic little wail.

In a voice she didn't recognise, she said, 'He looks better,' and tucked the shawl carefully around the little body.

Marc Corbett didn't take his eyes from the road. 'How's his breathing?'

Unevenly she said, 'Regular.' And, indeed, Brodie seemed to have slipped into a deep, natural sleep that was immensely reassuring.

'His colour?'

'Normal.'

She sneaked a rapid sideways glance. Bad move.

An ache rasped her throat and she turned her face resolutely to the front. Not fair, she thought fiercely. It simply wasn't fair that Marc Corbett should turn up when her life seemed to have crumbled into dust around her. It was a wonder he hadn't arrived in a clap of thunder, with lighting effects and a sinister laugh.

She knew that handsome face—the strong jaw and high cheekbones—as well as her own. Six years hadn't dimmed the brilliance of his eyes—a blue so intense they blazed with the colour and fire of sapphires. Looking into Marc Corbett's eyes was like being spun into the heart of an electrical storm.

How many times had she caught a glimpse of a tall dark

man and suffered this passionate, shameful excitement? Too many to count...

But until now it had never been the man she'd unconsciously been looking for; just as well, because six years previously he had married her childhood friend Juliette.

And two years ago Juliette had died in a tragic, senseless road accident. Paige's throat closed as she remembered the girl who'd been a charming substitute older sister to her.

The woman in the back seat leaned forward to say, 'Poor little boy! What is the matter with him? Do you know?'

She sounded so genuinely worried that Paige almost forgave her the sly comment about her being a horrible example.

Unevenly she answered, 'He's feverish and he has a rash; I think he might have chickenpox.'

But she couldn't banish the terrifying word *meningitis* from her mind.

She'd expected to have to repeat the directions to the surgery, but Marc Corbett didn't need his mind refreshed. As the building came into view, she said woodenly, 'You can stop here—pull left.'

'I know I am in New Zealand.' A faint, alien inflection to his intonation betrayed the influence of his French mother.

Without thinking, Paige turned her head. A royal blue gaze seared across her face before returning to the road.

Very appropriate! Royal blue eyes for a man who owned and ruled a commercial empire. Nerves wound tight in unbearable tension, Paige swallowed. Meeting Marc again had been a hideous, meaningless coincidence. He'd drop her off here and disappear from her life.

Which was exactly what she wanted.

The luxurious car drew into a miraculously empty length of kerbside. Anxiously searching Brodie's face, Paige wondered if Marc had ever had to search for a parking space like ordinary people. Probably not; his combination of ruthless determination and compelling charisma seemed to magic obstacles away.

'Thanks very much,' she said awkwardly, releasing herself from the seatbelt to scrabble for the door handle.

'Wait there.'

But as he strode around the front of the car she fumbled the door open. From the back came the woman's voice, amused yet chiding.

'It's best to do what he says. He's a very—dominant—man.'

She invested that word *dominant* with a lingering amusement that made Paige feel sick. If this was Lauren Porter, she was obviously still very much in Marc's life.

Why not? A man who'd maintained a mistress during the four short years of his marriage wasn't likely to let his wife's death break up the relationship.

When he opened the door Paige attempted to scramble out, but worry and shock made her awkward, and after a moment Marc plucked her and Brodie from the car with a leashed violence that destroyed the last pathetic shreds of her composure.

Once he was sure she was steady on her feet, he dropped his hands as though she'd contaminated them. 'Are you all right?'

His voice was cold and hard as iron, and as smoothly disciplined. Sensation flayed her with a diabolical combination of stimulation and fear—and, stronger than both, a weird, unnerving sensation of relief, as though she'd been lost and was now found again.

Clutching the baby, Paige stepped back and said tonelessly, 'Fine, thank you,' before racing into the sanctuary of the surgery.

While the woman at the counter pulled Brodie's records from the computer she turned her head and watched Marc's companion—slender, dressed in the signature good taste of a fashionable designer—ease gracefully into the front seat of the car with a flirtatious hint of long, superb legs. As soon as the door closed the vehicle pulled smoothly from the kerb and merged into the flow of traffic, disappearing almost immediately.

No doubt he was as glad to get rid of her as she was to see him go. A sour jab of disillusionment, goaded by that acute, painfully physical awareness, propelled Paige across to the waiting area.

She sat down in a chair apparently chosen for its lack of comfort and rocked a now wakeful—and very fretful—Brodie. Marc's companion fitted the description Juliette had given of a height to match Marc's six foot three or so. Even their colouring matched. Her black hair was cut into a style that suited her fine features. And Juliette had admired her eyes—'Grey as an English dawn,' she'd said.

The accent fitted too.

'She is English and clever—an executive in Marc's organisation. Marc says she is brilliant,' Juliette had told her, modern technology delivering the catch in her voice perfectly across the twelve thousand miles that had separated her from Paige. 'At least he doesn't shame me with his choice of a mistress; she is lovely and wears clothes like a Frenchwoman.'

Paige's knuckles gleamed white on the receiver. 'You might be getting it all wrong, you know. Unless—has he admitted it?'

'Oh, no.' Juliette sounded shocked. 'I am not going to ask him—I don't need to. I have seen them together, and that is enough. They are very discreet, but there is a connection between them that is impossible to miss.'

'What do you mean? Surely they don't—?'

'Flirt?' Juliette had sighed. 'Marc would never humiliate me like that. I can't describe the link between them except to say that it is there, like an invisible chain binding them together.'

And let's not go there now, Paige thought wearily, rocking the whimpering baby. Just concentrate on getting Brodie to the doctor, and working out how you can make your pathetic savings last until you get another job.

Half an hour later, when she walked out into the bright winter sunshine and heard a deep voice say her name, she wasn't surprised, although her heart contracted into a tight, hard lump in her chest. She'd known he'd be waiting for her.

'Did the doctor agree with your diagnosis of chickenpox?' he asked in a hard voice with a disturbingly abrasive undernote.

Warily she thrust the prescription into her jeans pocket as Brodie snuffled beneath the shawl. Although bright sunlight gilded the city, a sharp wind blustering in from the sea promised a cold night.

Marc was alone, she realised with humiliating relief. Not breaking stride, she returned in a tone as chilly as the air, 'Yes, she did. I'm sorry, I haven't time to talk. I need to fill a prescription and then take Brodie home.'

Marc fell in beside her, saying inflexibly, 'I'll drive you there.'

To a grotty little flat down an alleyway behind a hamburger joint? *Never.* She said quickly, 'It's all right; it's not far.'

'It's not all right. The child is ill.'

'The doctor was certain that it's the first stage of chickenpox, which is not a serious illness.' She paused, then said with a touch of malice, 'I hope you've had it. Chickenpox is very infectious.'

'I believe I had all the childhood diseases.' His hard, handsome face revealed nothing. 'Have you had it?'

'Juliette and I had it together,' she said stonily. 'I gave it to her, I believe.'

A rapid glance took in the symmetry of angles and planes in the outrageously good-looking face that radiated formidable, uncompromising power. His dead wife's name brought no flicker of remorse or sorrow.

She dragged her eyes away, but it was too late; he'd seen her survey him and something kindled in the depths of his striking eyes. His voice, however, was all controlled assurance. 'Nevertheless, I'll take you home. Give me the prescription form and you can wait in the car with the child.'

No doubt his formidable brain was slotting her involuntary response into a mental file. Marc Corbett hadn't turned a large family fortune into a stupendous one by the age of thirty-two without an incisive, analytical intelligence backed by relentless determination. He'd used his father's legacy to become a player on the world stage.

And he knew women.

Masking her jumping nerves with a frozen façade, she said crisply, 'Thank you, but you don't need to go to the trouble.'

The door to the pharmacy beckoned; she turned abruptly, feeling him follow her, noiseless and purposeful as a predator.

Which, she reminded herself, was exactly what he was. His father had been called the Robber Baron in the business press; no one dared whisper that about Marc, but she'd read enough to know that his name inspired respect mingled with fear.

Brodie began to cry again, his head turning restlessly inside the shawl. 'Hush, darling.' Paige juggled him as she fumbled in her jeans pocket. Her voice softened into a murmur. 'It's all right, sweetheart, you'll feel better once we get some of this stuff inside you.'

'Give him to me,' Marc commanded.

Shock whipped her head up; she looked directly into his autocratic face, its bold, chiselled features set in a mask of impatience.

'He doesn't like strangers,' she said raggedly.

One black, ironic brow shot up, and memories squeezed her heart painfully.

Marc said crisply, 'Then give me the prescription form.'

'I can manage.' But Brodie chose that moment to stiffen alarmingly.

Fortunately it didn't turn into another convulsion—it was only the prelude to a shriek. While she was hushing the baby, Marc gave her a glittering glance in which irritation and concern were blended, and before she had time to object his fingers had invaded her pocket and hauled out the piece of paper.

'Wait here,' he commanded, and strode up to the pharmacy counter.

Where, of course, he got instant service. Body throbbing at his unexpected touch, Paige's gaze followed him as she rocked the baby, trying to soothe him with softly spoken nonsense. Marc's overwhelming physical presence owed something to wide shoulders and lean hips and long athlete's legs, but more to an intangible aura of power and effortless authority that had cut a path through the other customers. Sensation twisted inside her, paradoxically sharp and smouldering.

And forbidden.

She noted with a pang of fear that inexplicable feeling

of rightness, as though the past six years had been a night-mare and she'd just woken to a new dawn. Don't be so ridiculous, she told herself staunchly. He's just like Dad. Marriage vows mean nothing.

Subsiding into whimpers, the baby stuffed a tiny fist into his mouth and sucked noisily until he realised he wasn't going to get nourishment from there. His desperate roars once more filled the pharmacy when Marc arrived back with the medication in one lean hand.

'Let's go before he eats that hand,' he said, turning with his other hand on her elbow, steering her out onto the footpath.

Paige didn't fool herself that she had any choices; for some reason Marc Corbett had decided he was going to take her home, and those fingers resting so casually on her arm would clamp if she tried to run. Although she hated to surrender, it meant nothing against the need to get the medicine and some liquid into Brodie immediately—and to ring Sherry, his mother, as soon as she could to reassure her that Brodie only had chickenpox.

Back in the car, with the lingering perfume of his previous passenger floating around her, Paige gave directions in a flat, remote voice. Sexy and modern, the scent breathed money and leisure and privilege, taunting her with its lazy exclusiveness.

She stiffened her shoulders and stared through the windscreen. It was difficult to find a dreary part of Napier, but today she saw her street with fresh eyes—the eyes of a man accustomed to the best. Subdued, out at the elbows, the collection of small shops and houses was only redeemed by bright flowers and shrubs.

'Number twenty-three,' she told Marc, the taste of defeat bitter on her tongue.

He turned down the drive between the fast food bar and an electrical goods shop that had seen better days.

'It's the second unit,' Paige said reluctantly.

The car drove down the row of cheaply built units; an elderly, failed motel had been turned into cramped apartments. Parking in the space allotted to her unit, Marc killed the engine.

Without taking his hands from the wheel, he surveyed the red-brick building with its aluminium ranch-slider windows and small concrete terraces separated by flower boxes. Most were desolate except for a few rugged weeds scraping an existence in dusty earth. Only the one outside Paige's unit radiated colour—brazen marigolds, their gold and lemon and rich mahogany defying the general hopelessness.

'Thank you,' she said levelly as Brodie, soothed into sleep by the motion of the car, woke with another weary little whimper. She wanted Marc out of there, safely banished to his world of luxury where the last thing *he'd* have to worry about was the state of his bank balance.

'Give the baby to me,' he ordered.

Startled, she said, 'I can manage.'

His beautiful mouth compressed into a thin line. 'It will be easier for you to get out if I have him.'

She hesitated.

'What are you afraid of?' he asked softly, blue eyes sardonic. 'That I'll kidnap him?'

'Of course not.'

'I won't drop him either.' His tone mocked her.

Flushing, she handed over the baby and leapt out of the car, only to see Marc emerge too, Brodie held with firm confidence in his arms. No stumbling or hesitation either, she noted; his distinctive ease and power made every movement graceful in a very masculine way.

'I'll bring him in,' he said, when she came towards him. 'You'll manage your keys more quickly if you aren't carrying him.'

Thus neatly forestalling her plans of taking the child and walking away, leaving him with no option but to drive off.

Not that he would have. Seething at her helplessness, Paige swung on her heel and walked across the bare concrete to insert the key with a vicious twist.

When she turned Marc was just behind her, and as she pushed the door back he walked in, dark head a few centimetres below the lintel, with Brodie traitorously silent in his arms.

Marc stopped in the middle of the threadbare carpet in all shades of mud, dwarfing the shabby, nondescript room. Paige burned with futile resentment as his narrowed, bright gaze checked out the elderly sofa, the table with two chairs—its scratched top covered by a sewing machine draped in a swathe of gleaming fabric—and the tiny kitchen overlooking a wall and a clothesline.

In spite of her efforts to cheer it up, she knew the room reeked with defeat. Not even the pots on the sill, fragrant with growing herbs, made any difference.

So what? she thought, stiffening her spine. She wasn't ashamed of living here.

He looked down at the baby in his arms, just as Brodie turned his head and sputtered a small amount of liquid over his shirt.

'Oh, I'm sorry,' Paige said, hoping her tone drowned out any defensive note as she came over and held out her arms for the baby. 'I'll take him now.'

'It's nothing.' Marc's voice was hard and autocratic, but when Brodie forced a small fist into his mouth and began to suck noisily his expression changed, some fugitive emotion softening the dominant features. 'I don't know much about children this small, but surely that indicates that he needs food?'

'He needs changing and medicine first. I'll heat a bottle,' she muttered unhappily, racing into the kitchen to grab a cloth and run it under the tap. She held it out to Marc, but he ignored it.

'I'll hold him until you've prepared it,' he stated, his pleasant inflection not hiding the steel in the words.

She did *not* care what he thought of her or the flat—not a bit. In fact, she was probably doing the world a service, showing him how the other half lived!

But the bitterness of rejection scraped across her skin. Stubbornly silent, she yanked open the refrigerator door and took out a sterilised bottle filled with formula. The electric kettle with its frayed cord spat sparks when she plugged it in.

'Be careful!' Marc snapped.

A knot somewhere inside her loosened a fraction, only to tighten again when he glanced at her. Above Brodie's wails, she said, 'It's all right; I'm used to it. All it does is spit.'

'It's dangerous.'

But not as dangerous as you, she thought angrily. And she couldn't afford a new one anyway.

A frown knotting his dark brows, Marc looked at the sewing machine on the table, and the swirl of bright fabric beside it. 'What the hell happened? When last I heard you and your mother were living with a cousin near a village called Bellhaven. You were working for him in his farm office.'

Juliette must have told him, and he'd remembered.

Then he killed the tiny flicker of warmth this had engendered by finishing abrasively, 'How did you get from there to a slum in Napier?'

Paige's chin jerked up. She stared at the kettle. 'This might be a slum to you, but most of the world would consider it basic but perfectly adequate,' she said politely. 'As for how I got here, that's simple. Lloyd, my mother's cousin, died and his farm was sold.'

He watched her with hooded eyes. 'When was this?'

'About a year ago. We moved to Napier because my mother thought it would be a good place to live.' She swallowed and finished in a flat voice, 'Unfortunately, for her it was a good place to die.'

'What happened?' he asked in an oddly gentle voice.

'She went for a walk along the beach and got caught by a rogue wave.'

'I'm very sorry,' he said. 'I know how close you were. When was this?'

Something in his tone—a touch of rare gentleness—made her blink ferociously. 'Five months ago.'

The silence was broken by the sound of the kettle boiling. Paige switched it off and poured the water into a jug.

Marc looked from her to the child in his arms. 'Where is the child's father?'

Until then it hadn't occurred to her that he'd think Brodie was *her* child. Which just shows what an idiot you are, she told herself wearily. One look at Marc and your mind turns into candyfloss!

Before she could tell him about Sherry and Brodie the baby broke the silence with a wail, and she said swiftly, 'He isn't here. I'll take Brodie now; he needs changing and some lotion on his rash to stop the itching.'

She bore him off through a door without a backward glance. Marc's mouth curved in a sardonic smile as she closed that door firmly behind her.

Clearly she wanted him in her home as little as he wanted to be there. At any other time he'd be ironically amused at how much she resented the outrageous coincidence of their meeting, and the fact that the baby's illness meant she'd had to rely on a man she viewed with wary distaste.

But one thought burned holes in his self-control: she didn't want him there, but every time he came near her she reacted like a cat faced with an unknown threat, spitting defiance and acute awareness.

CHAPTER TWO

A FIERCE, very male smile curling his mouth, Marc looked around the room. It must have been dingy indeed when Paige moved in, yet without spending much she'd made it as welcoming as it could be, given its depressing furnishings. He'd be prepared to bet that she had painted the walls the soft, buttery gold that both warmed and lightened the small room, and the touches of colour were hers too.

The pool of vivid material on the table caught his eye; he walked across to examine it.

It looked like a fancy dress costume, brief and shrieking with colour, but he recognised it for what it was—a costume intended to tease and titillate, designed to reveal its wearer's breasts and waist and legs.

So, Lauren had been right; as well as being a single mother and a woman down on her luck, Paige was a stripper or a lap dancer—or some such thing. Life hadn't been easy for her since her mother died; she had already developed the bright, hard shell of a woman who'd been rejected too often to trust any man.

Who the hell was her lover? Marc totted up months and realised that it had to be someone from Bellhaven. Why wasn't he here for Paige and his son?

Marc's lip curled with contempt as he thrust hands that bunched into fists in his pockets. He'd like to have the father of her child to himself for a few minutes, he thought with cold, aggressive anger; he'd show him exactly what he thought of a man who got a woman pregnant and then abandoned her.

But beneath the contempt was another, more primitive emotion—anger that some other man had taken the woman he wanted. Facing the admission with a slow burn of fury, he tried to rationalise this degrading infatuation.

It was nothing more than simple, basic lust, and if he gave it free rein it would reduce him to the same level as the men who paid to see her remove the cheap satin bra and scanty, high-cut briefs.

And although he mightn't be able to evict the mindless hunger from the weak part of him that bred it, he could certainly control it.

A memory leapt into his mind, shiny and precise as though it had been continually polished. They had danced at his wedding, the conventional dance of bridegroom and bridesmaid. He remembered the fresh, faint scent that had been hers alone, the way her slim body had moved against his with natural grace and an innocent seductiveness. She'd been seventeen, overwhelmed and excited, yet she'd glanced up through her lashes with a purely female need.

Desire gripped him, powerful, laden with temptation— and completely despicable.

She'd be a good stripper, he decided cynically. Not only did she move like a houri, but she looked like one—a walking, breathing challenge even now, when grief and pregnancy and sleepless nights with a sick child had leached much of the radiance from her fine, soft skin and ground away her vitality.

Nothing had been able to dim the rich honey glaze of her hair, or the gold lights in her great green eyes, or the full, sensuous contours of her mouth.

And she faced the world with a dogged independence that jutted her jaw and kept her shoulders squared.

In Sherry's bedroom, Paige fastened a clean napkin and manoeuvred Brodie into new leggings. The lotion she'd smoothed on seemed to have eased the itchy rash; he still wriggled, but without the frantic restlessness of a few minutes ago.

'Those red cheeks haven't gone away yet, though,' she murmured, kissing him as she picked him up. 'Better get some of that medicine inside you right now.'

But she had to force herself to take the first step towards the living room. No other man sent subtle electrical shocks through her with the accidental, meaningless brush of his skin against hers. Even in the dark she'd know Marc by his touch, she thought dazedly.

And he felt it too. Her spine had tingled when she'd seen the ruthless, swiftly concealed awareness in his eyes.

She wanted him and he wanted her.

Which was why she'd let him go on believing that Brodie was her child. Marc was no lover for a virgin to cut her teeth on.

What was he doing in Napier?

Not, she thought with bitter pragmatism, looking for her—when their eyes had duelled across the hotel foyer he'd been as astonished as she had.

And because that thought hurt much more than was safe, she went through the door and out into the cramped living room.

'I measured out the dose of medication,' Marc said, his voice cool and detached.

'Thank you.'

Brodie hated it; he spluttered and choked, thrusting out his tongue in disgust, but eventually she managed to get the drops into him.

Marc asked curtly, 'Why doesn't the baby's father live here?'

'He's in Australia.' She tested the temperature of the milk on her wrist. Exactly blood heat, so she carried both baby and bottle over to the shabby sofa. Deliberately she shook a swathe of hair across her face to serve as a fragile barrier against Marc's penetrating eyes.

'Are you joining him?' Marc asked, as though he had the right.

'No.' Keeping her eyes on the baby's face, she said neutrally, 'The rash looks much more like chickenpox now.'

Brodie began to suck with enthusiasm, but the milk didn't bring its usual satisfaction. After a few seconds he turned his head away and whimpered.

'Come on, sweetheart,' she encouraged him. 'You've got to get some liquid into you; you don't want to dehydrate.'

Achingly, violently aware of the man who watched her with a shuttered sapphire gaze, she risked a swift glance from beneath the curtain of her hair.

Apart from the hardening of his wide, sculpted mouth, no emotion showed in Marc's expression. Yet beneath the charismatic combination of tanned skin and brilliant eyes set off by hair as dark as sin she sensed cool speculation. Skin tightening, she shook her hair back and met his eyes.

With a brisk, no-nonsense emphasis, she said, 'Thank you. You've been very kind. Would you mind closing the door when you leave?'

The long, powerful muscles in his thighs flexed as he lowered himself onto the other end of the sofa.

'Tell me why you're living like this,' he said, a purposeful note in his voice making it more than clear that he had no intention of going until he'd got what he wanted.

Fighting back a rapid flare of resentment at his probing, she parried, 'Compared to the way some people live, this isn't bad.'

One black brow lifted in cool disbelief, but his voice

was perfectly courteous. 'You're being evasive. I presume your mother's death left you badly off financially?'

Her composure began to unravel. 'Funerals cost money.'

He was silent for a heartbeat. Quietly he said, 'Why didn't your cousin provide for you and your mother in his will?'

'Why should he? He had a son.' Paige knew her voice sounded flat, but she couldn't change it. She added, 'Lloyd was very good to us; he gave us a home for years.'

He didn't look convinced. 'Juliette said your mother kept house for him and you organised his books.'

Keeping her eyes on Brodie's face, Paige said quietly, 'He paid us.' Not a living wage, but they'd managed.

'Keeping you home was selfish of him and your mother,' Marc observed austerely. 'They should have sent you to university.'

Paige bit her lip. It seemed like a betrayal to be discussing her mother's tragic affliction with this man, intimidating in his strength and confidence. 'Mum needed me. After my father left us she suffered from bouts of depression.' Sometimes she had lain in bed for weeks at a time, staring into the grey world she'd inhabited.

Marc frowned. 'There are drugs available.'

'None of them worked.' Brodie snuffled a little and jerked his head around. As she coaxed him to drink some more Paige said, 'Anyway, we were happy here; it mightn't look much to you, but Mum settled in well. I got a job in an office and everything—everything seemed to be humming along. Then I was made redundant, and Mum died.'

She'd been so thrilled to get that job; her only employable skills were farm bookkeeping, and her previous experience didn't cut much ice. But she'd been given a chance and she'd been determined to make the most of it.

Then she'd discovered that her boss had a roving eye and hands that followed suit. An even greater blow to her pride followed: when she'd threatened him with a sexual harassment charge he'd let slip that he'd hired her because he'd seen her as an easy mark, a victim.

Well, she'd soon disabused him of that idea; startled by her angry response, he'd left her alone, but a month later she'd been made redundant. Yet another rejection, she thought cynically.

She hadn't been able to get another position. In summer there'd be plenty of casual work, but summer was several months off. No one wanted a woman with practically no employment history and a reference so subtly non-committal the only thing a prospective employer could take from it was that she'd been hopeless in the one job she'd had.

Marc looked at the pale, proud profile and swore silently in rapid French, deciding not to push further, although the green glitter in her eyes told him there was more to the story than that.

Had she been raped? The thought made him feel both sick and coldly, furiously angry. He didn't want to force her confidence; besides, there were other ways of finding out what he wanted to know.

'How long had your mother suffered from depression?' he asked casually.

'Since just after Juliette and her family went back to France.'

When that ironic brow shot up again she elaborated in an offhand voice, 'My father left us for his secretary. It shattered my mother.'

He frowned, eyes hard and blue as diamond shards. 'Are you in touch with your father still?'

She said briefly, 'He's dead too.'

'How long did you live next door to Juliette?' Marc asked with what sounded like idle interest.

Her expression softened. 'About eight years.' Juliette's father had been a diplomat, and in spite of the difference in their ages Juliette had been incredibly kind to her.

Marc leaned onto the painfully uncomfortable back of the sofa. It smelt clean, as did the unit, although a faint lingering taint in the air hinted at too many cigarettes smoked years ago, too much beer spilt on the thin carpet. He hated to see her in such surroundings.

Resisting any impulse to ask himself why, he said, 'What are your plans now?'

She skewered him with sword-points of green-gold fire. 'At the moment I have none beyond getting another job,' she said politely, setting the bottle down on the plywood table beside a small blue vase that held a single marigold, bright and flamboyant as the sun. She lifted Brodie and held him to her shoulder, patting his back until he brought up the last of his wind.

'Doing what?' When she didn't immediately answer he indicated a book on the floor by the sofa, a large tome she'd borrowed from the library written by a famous plantsman about his travels in search of new varieties. She'd been thoroughly enjoying it. 'I see you're interested in plants.'

'I like flowers. I find the whole business of breeding plants fascinating,' she said in a cool voice, silently mourning a lost dream. At school she'd planned to study botany and biology, and then work in a nursery. That had gone by the board when she'd realised that her mother couldn't cope without her.

Marc said calmly, 'Juliette would be upset to see you in such a situation.'

Didn't he realise that his unfaithfulness had distressed

Juliette infinitely more than anything else ever could? Outrage made Paige's reply brutal. 'I can manage. And Juliette has been dead for almost two years.'

'It was such a complete waste.' His voice was sombre, and when she looked up she saw his eyes close briefly.

But when he opened them again they were cold and clear and unreadable.

'Utterly,' Paige agreed unsteadily, deciding that he was an unfeeling, insensitive clod.

He'd rung her to tell her of Juliette's death; when she'd wept he'd been kind but icily remote.

She'd read more in the newspapers. Her friend had been in the back seat of a limousine inching up a steep mountain road in Italy. A truck with failed brakes had hurtled around a corner and pushed them off the cliff. Juliette, the chauffeur and the truck driver had died.

At least it had been immediate. Beyond one horrified second she'd probably not even known what had happened.

Blinking back tears, Paige coaxed a reluctant Brodie to accept more milk. He wriggled and turned his face sideways, before relenting and sucking again.

'I'm sorry. You must miss her too,' Marc said, his deep voice with its fascinating hint of an accent almost gentle. He touched her hand.

Paige's gaze flew to his face as that secret, blinding charge of electricity jolted her into a fiery oblivion where nothing else mattered but this man.

Before she could do anything stupid—like sighing or leaning towards Marc—Brodie gave a little choking splutter followed by an indignant wail.

Shaken, and intensely grateful to be saved from setting herself up for a rebuff, Paige lifted the baby and patted his back until he settled down. Marc Corbett belonged to a world as distant from hers as it was possible to be—a world of untold wealth, of power and privilege and social position.

He might want her, but the gap between them was impassable. Don't ever forget that, she told herself silently, tucking the bottle back into Brodie's mouth. He whimpered, spitting the milk out with disgust, and began to cry softly.

Accepting defeat, Paige got to her feet. 'He's ready for bed.' She looked directly at Marc, and her heart contracted in useless pain. 'Thank you for bringing us home,' she said formally.

He had risen when she did; she was tall enough, for a woman, but he towered over her, battering her with the power of his presence and his forceful personality.

'Can you get a babysitter for him?' he asked, long thick lashes narrowing his gaze.

She swallowed and banished a craven impulse to lick her lips. 'Why?'

'Answer me, Paige.'

She lifted defiant eyes. 'I don't have to answer you,' she said in a low, intense voice. 'I'm not your employee or someone who wants to curry favour with you. The question of a babysitter doesn't arise because I won't leave Brodie.'

Another evasion, but with any luck she'd made him angry enough not to notice. She turned away with the almost sleeping child in her arms and headed for the door that led to two small bedrooms and a minuscule bathroom.

Marc's voice came from behind, cool and deliberate. 'In that case, I'll come along tomorrow morning and bring breakfast for us both.'

Paige froze. 'No,' she said tautly.

'Why not?'

She was shaking her head, knowing only that she didn't dare see anything more of him. The only way she could think of to counter that inflexible will involved threatening him with harassment, and she couldn't trust herself to berate him without waking Brodie.

Fuming, she opened the door into the tiny hall. 'Because I don't want you here,' she said between her teeth.

'Tough,' he said, just as bluntly. 'We have things to talk about.'

She swivelled around. 'What on earth do *we* have to talk about? Juliette is dead, and she was the only thing we had in common.'

A sardonic brow lifted as he surveyed her with infuriating confidence. 'Unfortunately, that's not true. At the moment you're too concerned about Brodie to concentrate. He'll almost certainly be feeling much better in the morning and we can discuss things then.'

Paige pressed her lips together as he walked out into the sunshine and closed the door behind him.

Cradling the baby, she watched the sun strike fire from Marc's head. He seemed a creature from another planet—virile, radiating a potent energy that transformed the tired, drab surroundings and set her thrumming with deep, hidden desires.

Dangerous, frightening desires, doomed to be frustrated. She turned away, sickened by her body's treachery.

As she tucked the baby into his crib and stood patting his back, she thought of Juliette. It had been only a couple of years after her marriage that she'd rung Paige from New York and recounted her suspicions about Marc and Lauren, her lightly accented voice wry and steady.

Paige, her own life smashed to splinters after her father had walked out on her and her mother, had said immediately, 'Dump him.' And wondered why she'd felt so desolate.

But Juliette replied, 'That would be stupid. This is only a fling.'

Astounded, Paige said, 'But you'll never be able to trust him!'

'I trust him not to abandon me, as your father did your mother,' Juliette said with complete conviction. 'Marc won't betray me like that.'

And when Paige spluttered into silence her friend continued, 'He and I understand each other. He is not like your father and I am not like your mother, eating out my heart for something I can't have. We have a very good marriage, and if common sense and practicality sound a little boring, they are not such bad foundations for a union that will last a lifetime.'

'If that's the case, why are you upset about this affair?' Paige asked, honestly bewildered.

'Oh, it hurts a little.' Her friend gave a soft sigh. 'But I'm not all fire and passion, like you, and Marc and I came to an understanding of the sort of marriage we would have before we married. He was very honest.'

'He told you he'd have affairs?' Paige asked in shocked astonishment.

Where had Marc acquired such an arrogantly medieval attitude towards loyalty and honour in marriage? Surely Juliette didn't believe that it was merely a practical arrangement for the propagation of children and advancement of family fortunes?

Juliette laughed with real amusement. 'Of course not! He said he didn't seem able to feel the sort of love that poets write about, but that he liked me very much and wished for me to be the mother of his children. And I was glad, because between you and me, Paige, I'm not romantic either. I don't think I could cope with a *grande passion*; I've seen how they can tear people to bits, and they don't last. My children won't worry about their parents divorcing because one or the other falls in love with someone else. Marc and I will always be together, and there for them.'

Even now Paige could remember the shiver down her spine. Such a bloodless union might have suited Juliette, but she'd never accept so little from a man.

Actually, she had no intention of accepting anything from a man. Life without men was much more peaceful. She shuddered, recalling her mother's years of anguished despair after the break-up of her marriage. Laying yourself open to pain was foolhardy.

Voices from outside jerked her from her memories. With a final pat on Brodie's back, she hurried across to the window and peered through the curtains to see Sherry hurtle across the concrete, groping for her key as a taxi drew away.

By the time Paige got to the living room Brodie's mother had managed to unlock the door and was pushing it open, her small, voluptuous body quivering with frantic impatience.

'How is he?' she demanded.

Soothingly Paige told her, 'The doctor's sure it's chickenpox. I've put the prescription lotion on his rash and it doesn't seem to be worrying him nearly as much.'

'His temperature?' Sherry asked, rushing across to the door into the tiny hall.

'He's still flushed, but it hasn't been long since he took the medication.'

Sherry nodded and disappeared, leaving Paige listening to the low hum of a perfectly tuned engine. Her breath catching in her throat, she glanced through the window and saw the BMW turn back into the car park.

Incredulously she watched Marc get out, lift a parcel from the passenger's seat and walk purposefully towards the flat.

Mindful of Brodie, he knocked quietly. And it was only because she didn't want the baby to wake that she flew across to open the door. 'What do you want? I told you—'

He held out the parcel. 'Here.'

Paige stared at it with wary suspicion. 'What's that?'

'An electric kettle,' he told her, and strode past her and into the kitchen, where he dumped the parcel on to the counter.

White with temper, she gritted, 'I don't want it. Please go.'

'Not until I've collected this.' He picked up the old electric jug and its dangerously frayed cord. With a hard-edged smile he carried it across to the door.

Keeping her voice low, Paige said vehemently, 'I don't want anything from you.'

'Is it just me?' His eyes narrowed into steel-blue slivers. Into the heated silence he finished, 'That's the second thing you've refused to take from me.'

Paige's lashes flickered down over her eyes. 'I don't know what you mean,' she said in a wooden voice.

'You didn't want to accept the locket,' he said evenly.

She froze, and he smiled and touched her mouth with a long forefinger. Heat sizzled through her, and she clenched her eyes shut.

'That's not going to help,' he said with contempt. 'It's lust, Paige. ''The expense of spirit in a waste of shame,'' as Shakespeare said. We saw each other and we wanted each other, and neither of us can forget it.' He paused. 'Because it's still there.'

Her eyes flew open as the colour drained from her skin, leaving her cold and shivering. The anger and bitterness openly displayed in his face dried the words on her tongue.

His smile was savage. 'In spite of everything.'

And he kissed her, punishing her—and punishing himself too, she dimly realised as passion roared like a holocaust through her.

It only lasted a moment. He swore against her mouth, chilling words in a language she only dimly recognised to be French, and then let her go as though she disgusted him.

Swaying, Paige clutched the chair and watched him stride noiselessly out of the door.

Almost gibbering with a mindless mixture of rage and cold terror, she dammed the reckless words that threatened to tumble out and watched the car drive away, taking him out of her life.

'Wow!' Sherry breathed, easing herself around the door. 'And double wow. If any guy could make my little heart go pitter-patter again, it would be that one.'

'Don't even think about it,' Paige said furiously. 'There's a woman already in residence. She's tall and dark and super-elegant, and she suits him perfectly.' She dragged in a painful breath. 'Satisfied that Brodie's getting better?'

Sherry nodded. 'He's sound asleep.' She came across and looked at the parcel. 'What's this?'

'An electric kettle. Your triple wow of a man doesn't like ours.' Paige tried to smile.

'I don't blame him. Talk about living dangerously! What are you going to do with it?'

'Well, the original kettle belonged to you, so you choose.'

'Then I choose to keep it.'

Paige turned away, listening as Sherry unpacked the box. She felt as though her emotions had been flung into the heart of a cyclone and were whirling around in uncontrollable violence, destroying everything in their path.

'It's a good one. I'll christen it with a cup of coffee for us both,' Sherry said on a sigh. 'It's been a bastard of a day and I could do with something to give me some zip.'

Collapsing onto the sofa, Paige decided she could do with some extra zip too. Her mouth stung from Marc's kiss and she felt like a stalk of overcooked asparagus. This, she decided, must be an adrenaline crash.

CHAPTER THREE

SHERRY looked across the counter. In an elaborately casual voice she asked, 'Who was the guy?'

'My best friend's husband.'

'The friend who was killed in a car accident?' At Paige's nod her eyes widened. 'The French guy?'

'His mother is French,' Paige said scrupulously. 'His father was a New Zealander; they used to call him the Robber Baron.'

'This one looks pretty French to me.' Sherry filled the new kettle. 'Mediterranean macho to the nth degree. What do they call *him*? Lord of all he surveys?'

'It fits,' Paige told her with an acid smile, 'but I think they take him too seriously to call him anything but sir.'

'So what's he doing here? Did he come looking for you?'

Paige snorted. 'Why would he do that? It was sheer coincidence that we met in the foyer of the hotel. Don't worry; we won't be seeing him again.'

'You met him coming down from the club?' Sherry looked unhappily at her. 'I hope you told him you aren't a stripper—that you're just looking after Brodie for me until you get another job?'

'I didn't tell him anything because it's none of his business,' Paige said firmly. 'And I'm really sorry I had to visit you at work. I hope your boss wasn't too angry, but Brodie got sick so quickly. He was fine when I went down to pay the rent, but we were only halfway home when I could see he had a temperature, and I didn't have enough money to take him to the doctor.'

'Oh, the boss was a bit snippy, but she's got kids of her own so she understood. She let me off early without squealing.' Yawning, Sherry poured water into two mismatched mugs and brought one across to Paige.

Who sighed and asked, 'Why don't you give up stripping? You hate it and—'

'I'll give it up when I've paid off the debts my rat of a husband ran up in my name and when I've saved enough money to make a future for Brodie,' Sherry said firmly. 'I'm not brainy, like you. All I've got to offer is a good body and a sense of rhythm. Where else would I get decent money unless I worked the streets? And I'm not going to do that.'

Paige grimaced. 'Of course you won't.'

'Bloody men,' Sherry said, lowering herself onto the sofa. 'I'll bring Brodie up to think a lot more highly of women than his conman of a father ever did, I can tell you.' She glanced down at her finger, as though remembering the wedding ring that had once been there. 'He's going to be educated. He won't mortgage the house and gamble it away, then skip to Australia when he's found out.'

Paige raised her coffee mug. 'Here's to responsible men,' she said mockingly.

'I'll drink to that.'

But both women laughed.

Much later, as the sleepless night stretched before her, Paige lay in bed and deliberately let herself recall the first time she'd met Marc Corbett.

Only seventeen, she'd been so giddy with excitement she'd hardly been able to put two coherent thoughts together. With Juliette's bombshell request to be her brides-maid had come an invitation to her mother and first-class tickets to Paris. Although her mother had refused to travel, Lloyd had insisted that Paige go, offering to pay her expenses.

She thought now that she'd have been safer staying in her pleasant pastoral sanctuary at Bellhaven.

Yet it had all started so well. After the reunion with Juliette she'd discovered that their friendship still held. And then—oh, Paris! She'd loved the fittings for her gorgeous dress, the art galleries, the museums, the wonderful gardens—especially the gardens! Thoughtful as ever, Juliette had organised visits to several.

Marc had been on a business trip in Asia, not returning until two days before the wedding. They had met at a chic private dinner put on by his even more chic mother in her splendidly opulent apartment.

Introduced by a proud Juliette, Paige had looked into his remote, handsome face with sharp awareness and a terrifying, heated interest. Bewildered by the intensity of her response, she'd been formal and quiet, hoping that no one had noticed.

Restlessly Paige turned over in the bed and opened her eyes. Lights flashed across the window as a car rumbled into the forecourt, its engine kicking oddly before it died. Its door thudded shut, followed by the front door of a unit. Somewhere towards the port a siren sounded, eerily discordant.

In Paris the bridal party had stayed in a hotel, and after Marc had brought them back from his mother's dinner party Paige had gone to her room, tactfully leaving him with his fiancée.

But about half an hour later he'd knocked on the door.

When she'd opened it her silly heart had looped a wild circle in her chest.

'I think you should have this tonight,' he said, holding out a small, exquisitely wrapped parcel. 'As you are to wear it tomorrow.'

Eyeing it, she said wonderingly, 'What is it?'

His smile melted her spine. 'It's traditional for the bridegroom to give the bridesmaid a gift,' he told her. And when she didn't reach for it he said a little impatiently, 'This is it.'

Almost reluctantly she took the small parcel, flushing because her hand shook when his fingers touched hers. 'Thank you,' she half-whispered, mortified by the small betrayal.

She should have closed the door then, and opened the gift in her room, but by then she'd already started fumbling with the bow and the ribbon, so acutely conscious of him watching her that she felt he could see her forbidden excitement.

It was a jeweller's box. Paige's breath stopped in her throat. All she could hear was the feverish tattoo of her heart as she flicked it open.

It dazzled her with its beauty—a round gold pendant on a heavy gold chain, the link set with a diamond that flashed and gleamed as blue as his eyes.

'It's perfect,' she said huskily, keeping her head down. 'Thank you so much.'

'It's a locket,' he told her. 'For keeping pictures of one's lovers.' His voice deepened. 'Or one particular lover.'

Heat flamed through her. 'Thank you,' she said again, because she couldn't find any other words.

Silence, thick and pulsing with hidden intensity, linked them in a frightening cell of intimacy.

Marc broke it with a quick, harsh question. 'Are you going to put it on?'

She hesitated, then took the lovely thing from the velvet box and looped it around her neck. Every tiny hair on her body stood upright; her skin, oddly too tight, prickled with sensation as she fumbled the catch.

'Turn around,' Marc told her, that note of impatience roughening his voice again.

Mouth dry, she obeyed, and he did it up, his fingers cool on the nape of her neck. Excitement rode her hard with a jolt of pure fusion—fire and ice and a rushing thrill that almost overwhelmed her.

'There,' he said, his voice oddly clipped, and stepped back.

Slowly, afraid of what she might see in his face, she turned towards him. He looked at the locket against her skin.

'Very pretty,' he said distantly, his voice as steady as his eyes. But in his jaw a muscle flicked once, twice, three times.

'Thank you,' she said, a cold unease spreading beneath her ribs. She didn't know how to close this, so she gave a brief, meaningless smile and stepped back, shutting the door against him and leaning back on it with her stomach lurching.

He had looked at her as she had seen her father look at the woman he'd left her mother for. And, although Paige was a virgin, she'd seen enough of illicit desire to recognise its heavy, ominous throb.

Snatching off the locket, Paige dropped it into the box and snapped it shut, horrified by the sensations rioting through her—an aching sweetness and a reckless urgency that made her breasts tingle and her body throb.

Sick at heart, she despised herself. Tomorrow Marc was

going to marry her best friend, but for a moment she'd wanted him with a desire that scared her witless. A few words, a touch, an exchange of glances had been all it took to transmute her innocent awareness into a heated, urgent need.

For the whole of the next day, the locket that Juliette insisted she wear burned like fire against her skin.

A month later, Paige staggered out of bed and struggled into her clothes before tiptoeing past Sherry's firmly closed door. Brodie's chickenpox was now a dim memory, and although he'd graduated to sleeping right through the night, she didn't want to disturb either him or his mother.

Paige glanced at her watch. He usually didn't stir until the shift worker next door slammed his car door and revved out of the car park. She had a bit more than an hour to do her part-time job and pick up the newspaper so she could scan the situations vacant.

She fought back a clutch of panic; although she wasn't any closer to finding a job, she could now claim the dole. However, that wouldn't be enough to pay Sherry back for the last three weeks' rent, so Paige was now walking two dogs every morning from Monday to Friday.

It helped, but not enough. If she couldn't get a job, she'd have to leave; Sherry couldn't afford to keep supporting her, even if she did look after Brodie in return. Her own dreams had been put on hold; she wasn't going to shatter Sherry's.

Her charges, a large German Shepherd and a vigorous Jack Russell, welcomed her with their usual seething energy; once in the park she threw a ball for them to scrap over.

When they'd worked off most of their high spirits they set off along the riverbank, the Jack Russell making eager forays into the scrub after rabbits, the gentler German Shepherd bitch at Paige's heel, except for occasional side trips when a particularly exciting smell seduced her.

Fortunately they kept her busy enough supervising so that her brain couldn't wander in forbidden directions. As swiftly as he'd appeared Marc had dropped out of her life. A note the day after they'd met had explained that he'd been called overseas on business and he was hers, Marc.

Not that she'd expected to see him again, but she'd been furious with herself for the terrible desolation that had swept over her. He meant nothing to her, and he couldn't have made it more obvious that she meant nothing to him.

Which was just the way she'd expected things to be.

The wind, cooled by thousands of miles of southern ocean, pounced onto her, flattening the thin material of her jersey against her skin. She firmed her mouth against a shiver. Unfortunately, her recovery from the shock of his arrival wasn't helped by his appearance every night in her dreams.

The sudden alertness of the bigger dog, followed almost immediately by an aggressive fusillade of barking from the smaller, swivelled her head around. A man was striding towards her from the direction of the road, his long legs covering the ground with rapid efficiency.

Pulses leaping, she faltered, then stopped. Tall, dark and dominant, it could only be Marc. Talk about the devil...!

For one horribly embarrassing moment she found herself wishing she'd worn something better than threadbare jeans and an elderly jersey that matched the colour of her eyes but had long since seen off its better days.

Then embarrassment was banished by a disturbing jolt of energy that jump-started both her heart and her breathing.

So much for getting over it, a small inner voice jeered silently.

'Sit,' she said sharply as the dogs danced protectively around her. When they'd obeyed she turned to face the man striding towards her, shoulders squared, jaw jutting at a deliberate angle.

Her stomach contracted as though expecting a blow. He wasn't smiling, but she sensed a leashed satisfaction behind the impassive mask of his face. It was unfair that the sun should bronze his aquiline features with such besotted accuracy. Goaded, she lifted her head so high her neck muscles began to protest, and directed a carefully cool gaze at him.

He said, 'Are you all right?' When she stared blankly at him, he said, 'Sherry said you'd had the flu. What the hell are you doing walking dogs on these cold mornings?'

Rallying her defences, Paige returned, 'I'm better now.'

'You don't look it,' he said bluntly, surveying her with a hard blue gaze. 'You're pale and you've got great dark circles under your eyes.'

When he'd first met her she'd been a glowing, sensuously vibrant girl, her warmth reflected in her skin and dark honey hair, in the green-gold depths of her large, black-lashed eyes. A month ago she'd been tired, but now—now, he thought forcefully, she looked like a woman whose reserves had been plundered too often—fragile, strained and exhausted. An inconvenient protectiveness stirred to life in him, followed by a deep, uncompromising anger.

'It was a nasty virus, but I'm feeling a hundred per cent better than I did this time last week,' she said stiffly, and clenched her teeth on another shiver.

'You shouldn't be out in this cold wind.'

He stripped off his jacket and, before she realised what

he was doing, slung it around her shoulders, turning her to wrap it around her. The body heat still clinging to the leather enveloped her, bringing a rapid lick of fire scorching up through her skin.

'I don't—' she muttered, trying to shrug the jacket from her shoulders.

Hard hands clamped it on. He said in a voice that sent shocks charging through her veins, 'If you don't keep it on, I'll pick you up and carry you back to the car.'

Even if she hadn't glanced into his unyielding face, she'd have known by the tone of his voice that he meant it. And the jacket was wonderfully warm, faintly scented with a fragrance that was as natural as his warmth.

Awkwardly, she muttered, 'Thanks. What are you doing here?' She stopped, the colour fading as she met eyes as cold and blue as polar ice.

He'd met Sherry.

Her gaze slid sideways. Then she rallied. 'I hope you didn't wake Sherry and Brodie.'

'They were already awake,' he said indifferently. 'I'm glad to see Brodie is over his chickenpox.'

Baffled, she said, 'He's fine. Why did you come back?'

'I told you last time. We have things to discuss.' The silky note in his voice tightened her skin.

'And I told you we have nothing to discuss,' she returned, her voice cold and remote, her eyes hard. 'We belong to different worlds.'

'If you believe that you're deliberately deluding yourself. But you don't believe that.' His words were cool and deliberate, at odds with the formidable aura he projected.

The Jack Russell growled.

Paige said sweetly, 'Tiger is an attack dog.'

Correctly judging the smaller dog to be the natural pack

leader, Marc held out an authoritative hand, letting it and then the German Shepherd sniff his fingers.

To Paige's irritation it was obvious that they accepted him as an Alpha male. After polite nasal inspections of the hems of his trouser legs, both sat down and panted cheerfully at him, tongues lolling.

He read Paige's expression correctly. Still in that smooth tone, he said, 'I like dogs; I have one of my own. Why did you deliberately let me think Brodie was yours?'

Paige shook her head. 'You didn't ask,' she pointed out, hoping her low voice hid the clammy pool of dismay beneath her ribs.

She didn't want him here, especially not in Napier, but even somewhere in the same country was too close. Why didn't he go back to the château in France, or the huge New York apartment, or the gracious Georgian house in London—anywhere but New Zealand?

He was too much, and the reactions she'd managed to ignore during the past month had exploded into life again.

'Why do he and his mother live with you?' For a moment she considered telling him to mind his own business, but he said satirically, 'I'm sure that if I offered Sherry a big enough sum of money she'd tell me.'

'How lucky you are to be overbearingly rich and famous,' she purred, her wits revitalised by another swift surge of adrenaline.

At this rate she'd overdose on it, but she'd shaken off the lethargy and depression that had followed her bout with the flu. Why had it taken this man, one she despised, to make her feel alive again?

'It's one of the perks,' he agreed without shame. 'Well?'

Marc decided that the insolent composure with which she met his lifted brows was a challenge in itself—one he was finding it more and more hard to resist.

She said with delicate scorn, 'Offer Sherry money to tell you, then. She needs it.'

Marc almost smiled. He never knew what she was going to say; the unexpectedness of her reactions was refreshing and intriguing. 'Why did you let me think that you were a stripper?'

'Because it was none of your business whether I was a stripper—or even a horrible example,' she returned crisply.

He frowned, recalling Lauren's teasing question in the foyer of the hotel. 'She didn't know you could hear.'

'I know. It's a quirk of acoustics.' Paige shrugged and called the restless dogs to heel. 'It doesn't matter—she's entitled to her opinion, even though she's pretty quick to judge.'

True, but he hadn't come to talk about Lauren. 'Last time I was here something blew up and I had to leave before I'd planned to. It took longer than I expected, but I always intended to come back. We do need to talk, Paige.'

'No.'

Marc noted absolute determination in her slender spine, straight and strong as steel reinforcing. This, he thought, with the relish he usually brought to boardroom battles, was going to be a fight—one he'd enjoy winning.

Which meant taking her by surprise. She was braced for battle, so he said, 'I'm calling this off. You're not making much of a fist of hiding those shivers.'

He whistled at the dogs. Maddeningly, both frisked towards him as if pulled by invisible strings. Made temporarily witless by such highhanded tactics, Paige even passed over the leashes when he held out a peremptory hand for them, watching with increasing resentment as he hooked on each dog with efficiency and speed.

Determined not to give in so easily, Paige glanced at

her watch. 'It's time we turned back, anyway,' she said, knowing it was surrender. Whether she wanted to go back or not, Marc was the one in control here.

White teeth flashed in an ironic smile. 'I'll go with you.'

'The dogs are my responsibility.' She held out her hand for the leashes.

Nodding, he gave them to her, then set off beside her, his tall, lean, graceful body shielding her from the sharp nip of the wind. Not that much got through his jacket, but his consideration made her melt inside.

It wasn't personal, she told herself scornfully. He'd do it for any woman.

Her senses seemed to have sharpened; the sun beat more warmly on her skin and the grass glowed iridescently green, while she was sure she hadn't ever noticed the faint, evocative perfume of some flowering plant before. Even the birds called with a more seductive sweetness.

Stop it! she commanded her traitorous body. Last week had been the second anniversary of Juliette's death; if he'd thought about her at all he could have found her any time in those two years. He'd have only needed to tell someone, Find this woman, and it would have been done.

But he hadn't done it. Keep that in mind, she told herself grimly.

After a few steps she asked, 'Where's your car?'

Walking beside him was boosting this terrifying, tantalising tension. She needed to stride out briskly and clear her mind of the fumes of desire summoned by the heady chemistry of his smile.

'Over by the road.' He nodded at a shape in the distance.

Baffled, she tamped down her anger and decided to make the best of the situation. 'All right, tell me whatever it is you want to—now.'

'Very well.' He sounded amused, but the humour left his voice with his next words. 'Juliette left you a legacy.'

She stopped abruptly. 'What?'

Long fingers around her elbow urged her on. 'In her will she left you a box. I don't know what it is. She also left you a sum of money.'

'I see,' she said colourlessly.

She pulled free of his grip, but she thought she could still feel the imprint of his fingers traced in molten outline on her skin. Oh, yes, right through your jersey and shirt, she scoffed, struggling to keep her equilibrium in a world suddenly tumbled off its axis.

'It's very kind of you, but you didn't have to come all the way here to tell me about Juliette's legacy,' she returned with crisp brevity. 'You can post the box to me. And I don't want any money. Give it to charity.'

'Ungracious as well as stubborn,' he observed in a pleasant tone that barely hid his contempt.

She stiffened. 'I'm not—I didn't mean to sound like that.' He waited in aloof silence until she finished lamely, 'I assume the box is a memento. I'd like that very much. But not money.'

'One comes with the other, I'm afraid,' he said flatly. 'And there are conditions.'

One simmering glance at his unyielding face told her he wasn't going to move on this. And that she wasn't going to like the conditions. 'What are they?' she asked, forcing the words out between her gritted teeth.

'Come to breakfast with me and I'll tell you.'

'Why can't you tell me here?'

He lifted his brows. 'Because you're already cold,' he pointed out. 'You're shivering, and your lips are starting to turn blue. And because Juliette's bequest deserves more than a few words exchanged in a park. I'd have thought you felt the same. Although you didn't see anything of each other in the last few years of her life, I know she kept in touch; I think in many ways you were her best friend. Is it too much to ask that you give me time to tell you about this?'

She went white. 'That's unfair and manipulative,' she flung back at him.

His broad shoulders lifted. 'The truth can't be manipulation,' he said, without giving an inch.

After a short hesitation she muttered, 'Oh, all right. I have to drop the dogs off, but I'll be at the flat in twenty minutes.'

'I'll take you and the dogs back,' he said implacably.

And, in spite of everything she could say, ten minutes saw both dogs transported to their home and Paige back at the flat.

When she emerged from the quickest shower she'd ever had, she could hear conversation in the living room—or rather she heard Sherry laughing over Marc's deep tones. Biting her lip, she took down a pair of chocolate-brown trousers and topped them with a corduroy shirt in a shade of spicy red that flattered her hair and her skin. Because the shower hadn't been able to warm her completely, she wore a creamy-white turtleneck beneath the shirt.

Lipstick gave her pale face a bit of warmth, but she still felt like something discovered under a stone—no fit state to have breakfast with Marc Corbett.

And, she thought masochistically, about as far removed from his original companion as anyone could be. In fact, the woman's scarf had probably cost more than her entire wardrobe was worth.

Not that Paige cared.

Yet she went out with a cake-mixer churning in her

stomach and had to force her face into an expression of
cool disinterest as she came through the door.

Marc's vitality hit her like a blow to the solar plexus.

His uncomfortably perceptive eyes blazed and his mouth
relaxed into a smile that held more than a hint of mockery.
Casual though his clothes were, Paige recognised the superb tailoring that covered broad shoulders and long legs
with loving fidelity.

He was—overpowering. The first time she'd met him
she'd sensed the heat that smouldered behind the cool restraints of his will power—sensed it and been scared by
it.

It was still there, and she was still afraid.

But she was more afraid of the excitement infiltrating
her body, heating into a subtle arousal, as they said their
goodbyes to Sherry and went out to the car.

CHAPTER FOUR

ONCE in the passenger's seat, Paige pasted a brittle skin over her turbulent emotions. 'It's going to be a glorious day when this wind dies down.'

'How long is it since you've had the flu?'

So much for the cheering effect of a bright shirt and some lipstick. 'Surely I don't look that bad?' she retorted.

And immediately clamped her lips in disbelief. Oh, what an opening! Marc took it, too, examining her from the top of her head to the hands that linked so tensely in her lap.

'You look as though you haven't fully recovered,' he said calmly, twisting the key. The engine purred into life, soft as the sound of luxury—yet, like its driver, it reeked of dangerous, barely curbed power. 'Sherry told me that you wouldn't let her call the doctor.'

'Doctors can't do anything for viruses,' she returned, wishing her flatmate had kept her mouth shut.

Efficiently backing the car out, Marc said with a touch of irritation, 'They can prescribe medication for any complications.'

'I didn't have any. It was just plain old ordinary flu—nasty, like flu always is, but I've recovered.'

After a stiletto-sharp, disbelieving glance, he commented, 'It's good to see little Brodie looking so much better.'

Welcoming a neutral subject, Paige said, 'The medication worked fast; he didn't have another convulsion and you guessed right—he was much better the next day.'

The big car moved smoothly out onto the street. A few

51

hundred metres later, Marc said coolly, 'I gather you've been looking after him while Sherry works?'

'Yes.'

'What hours?'

'From the middle of the afternoon to whenever she comes home.' Her voice was stiff and prickly.

'Every day?'

She shook her head. 'She has two days off each week.'

To her relief he didn't speak again until he'd parked the car outside a house up on the Port Hill.

'I thought we were going to a restaurant,' she objected, looking around with suspicion she didn't try to hide.

'I'm staying here,' he said laconically.

With his girlfriend? 'In a *house*?'

'Hotels bore me. I prefer being with friends.'

A cold emptiness expanded under her ribs.

His glance sliced through her. 'Paige, I'm not planning to murder you and tip you over the cliff,' he said, each word an exercise in icy precision. 'If you don't want to eat here I'll take you to the nearest restaurant and we can talk about Juliette's legacy in front of anyone who's interested.'

Murder had been the last thing on her mind, but she was being stupid; Marc was too worldly—and had far too much self-control—to give in to any wild clamour of the senses.

It was her own responses she was afraid of. However, as she certainly wasn't going to fling herself into his arms and pant, Take me! she'd be safe enough.

But she continued, 'What about your friend—the person who owns the house? I haven't been invited.'

'They're not here at the moment.' His hooded blue glance skimmed her face. 'They work. They know that you're coming to breakfast, and if it makes you feel better

I'll take you to meet them on the way home and introduce you.'

He sounded thoroughly fed up. 'That won't be necessary,' Paige said uncomfortably, and at last got out.

She could just imagine what his friends would be like—Hawke Bay aristocracy, with children who went to exclusive and expensive boarding schools and a circle of friends as sophisticated as Marc.

Sure enough, the house was luxurious—and superbly decorated. A crawling tension knotted her stomach as he escorted her into a dining room filled with sun and reflected light from the sea below.

'Sit down,' he said, indicating a table set with cheerful napkins and china. 'You look as though you could do with a jolt of caffeine.'

Once she was seated he brought in toast, fruit, porridge and coffee and juice, moving with the confidence of someone who had done this frequently.

Surprised, because she'd understood from Juliette that they had lived in some state—even his New Zealand home in the Bay of Islands had a resident housekeeper—Paige managed to eat a piece of toast and sip orange juice while he demolished a plate of porridge.

With a swift quirk of his lips he said, 'My father was one of the old school—he firmly believed that a man couldn't work on anything other than a plate of porridge.'

She smiled. Clearly robber barons had traditional tastes. 'Mine loved sausages and bacon.' Her mother had tried to convince him that he'd die of a heart attack. And he had.

But not until he'd been long gone from their lives.

Marc's sharp scrutiny sent a swift jab of sensation up her spine, but he began to discuss the upcoming election and she relaxed—as much as it was possible when she felt as nervous as though she was perched on the lip of an active volcano.

Eventually he said without preamble, 'The box Juliette left you is at Arohanui, my home in Northland. In her will she asked that you come to the island and collect it. She wanted you to stay a week there.'

Paige was already shaking her head. 'No,' she said huskily. 'It's impossible.'

'Why?'

Impatiently she retorted, 'I have to look after Brodie.'

He drank from his cup of coffee then set it down. 'Is that the only reason? Do you have someone who'd object? If so, bring him.'

Paige flushed. 'There's no one,' she said shortly, secretly resenting his indifference at the idea of her with another man. 'Brodie's the main reason I can't come, but I also walk the dogs every morning. You'll have to post it to me.'

'It's not that easy.'

Her voice settled into syrupy sweetness. 'It's not too hard to post a parcel, you know. You just wrap it up— possibly the housekeeper could do that for you—and take it to a post office. They'll do the rest.'

'Provocation isn't going to get you anywhere,' he drawled. 'The dogs and Brodie can be taken care of.'

Paige looked at him with simmering dislike. 'I've no doubt you can do that, but I need to earn some money until I get a job.'

'Do you have any interviews scheduled?'

'No,' she admitted reluctantly. 'Still, I'm not going to find jobs in Napier advertised in the local newspaper in the Bay of Islands!'

'I can organise that too,' he said casually. 'Most of the local papers will be on the Internet; if they're not, I'll get someone down here to look at the Sits Vac while you're away. Juliette wanted you to come up to Arohanui, and I think it's the least you can do for her.'

Paige bit back caustic words. *And your mistress? Will she be there too?*

Instead she spread her hands in bewilderment. 'What made her think of leaving me something? She couldn't have had any idea that...that she was going to die so tragically.'

'I insisted she made a will after we were married,' Marc said evenly. 'As for leaving you a memento—why not, for a friend she loved dearly? It's often done.'

She peered up through her lashes, saw his tanned skin tighten over the thrusting bone structure beneath. He looked completely self-assured, but his eyes were sombre beneath their heavy lids.

Reluctantly she accepted that although he might have hurt Juliette, he could miss her and grieve for a life cut so unfairly short.

The taste of coffee bitter in her mouth, Paige said, 'I didn't expect anything from her.'

'I know. And if you're wondering why you weren't told of this sooner, she specifically stated that her bequest not be given to you until two years after her death.'

Startled, she glanced at his face, met eyes as coldly crystalline as the blue depths of a glacier.

'Why?' she asked blankly. 'It seems odd to wait for two years, then ask me to go to Arohanui. She wasn't a person to indulge in whims, and she didn't even like—'

'The island? I know.' He lifted his shoulders in an eloquent shrug. 'She would have had a reason. Unfortunately, I have no idea what it was. But I intend to see that her wishes are met.'

Paige stared at the lazily swirling surface of her coffee.

Some part of her wished violently that Juliette hadn't remembered her like this. 'Do you know what it is, whatever she left me?'

One black brow shot up. 'No. It's small, so I suspect it's a piece of jewellery or some keepsake.'

'I can't afford to go,' she said baldly. 'I mean it; I haven't got the money to get there or home again.'

'That isn't relevant.'

She bristled. 'I don't want charity.'

Marc fixed her with another frigid shaft of ice-blue. 'She wanted to give you this,' he said, crushing and blunt. 'Is it too much of a sacrifice? A week of your time to fulfil the last thing she will ever ask of you?'

Paige scrambled to her feet and faced him across the table. 'You're a devious, manipulative swine,' she whispered.

He rose also. 'But you already knew that,' he said, his courteous tone a more pointed sword than any insult.

'I know exactly what you are,' Paige said between her teeth.

With a contemptuous smile Marc returned, 'Whatever you think of me, be assured that I have enough self-control not to force myself on women who don't want me.'

'I—I don't think…I mean, I wasn't thinking of that,' she said huskily.

But she had been, and he knew it. Humiliation ate into her composure; she was being ridiculous, because although he might find her attractive his self-control was legendary. She was making too much of this fierce awareness; what did she know about sex? Or the relations between the sexes, come to that? Her last boyfriend had been at high school, and she was that rare and exotic creature, a twenty-three-year-old virgin whose experience was confined to a little mild groping and a few enthusiastic but innocent kisses.

Marc was probably laughing at her.

He said calmly, 'If it makes you feel more confident, I plan to fly to Australia the day after I drop you off at the island.' He watched her with narrowed, piercing eyes, yet his voice warmed into a reassurance that sapped her will. 'Paige, please come up to Arohanui. I'll fly you up, and you can come back any way you choose to travel.'

Marc examined her pale, set face, despising himself because a ruthless need burned beneath the honest desire to do this last thing for Juliette.

A sardonic twist to his lips matched his emotions. He could do this; he could master his hunger.

Even as he monitored Paige's face for clues to her decision he was wondering what made him want her. Something subtler, more enigmatic than beauty, although his eyes appreciated skin like satin and the fine regular features that weren't particularly memorable—if you excluded green-gold eyes on a tantalising tilt, and a very determined chin.

Not to mention a lush mouth that beckoned with sultry promise in spite of its tight discipline, and a body that hinted of sensuous delights—slender and lithe and rounded. He tried to ignore the inconvenient stirring in his loins.

She was no push-over, but at the moment her defences were almost breached; she looked exhausted, and he resented the protective feeling that gripped him again.

'Don't make a big deal out of it,' he said, and took her cold hands in his, producing his trump card. 'I don't know why Juliette made it a condition that you come up to Arohanui, but as she did I'd like to see that her wishes are carried out.'

She shivered, shadows darkening her eyes to a defeated green as she lowered her lashes and looked away, and he knew he had her.

Pulling her hands free, she walked across to the window, her jerky movements revealing her agitation. When she turned back to face him he couldn't see her expression against the brilliance of sky and sea outside, but the tension in her shoulders told him she'd made a decision.

'All right,' she said, reluctance flattening her voice, 'but I'll have to organise things. I'm not going if Sherry can't get the time off to look after Brodie.'

Marc reined in a surge of satisfaction that eroded his control. 'I can help there.'

She gave him a slanting, rebellious look, but said with polite dismissal, 'Thank you, but that won't be necessary.'

A realist, and more than a little cynical, Marc knew that even without his wealth he'd be attractive to the opposite sex, so he was accustomed to women who looked at him and saw the promise of security. Or, at the very least, relished the prospect of fattening their bank balance while enjoying sex with him.

It was, he admitted wryly, unusual to have a woman treat him with barely concealed distrust. Was that why she was such a challenge?

No, he wasn't that cynical—or that shallow. For some reason she intrigued him at a primal, gut level that had the power to overthrow the checks and restraints he'd imposed on his passions.

'We'll see,' he said levelly. 'Now, I'm going to have bacon and eggs. Would you like to join me?'

Paige was astonished to feel her stomach growl softly in response. 'I—thank you.'

'Sit down and I'll bring some through—or you can come and watch me cook, if you like.'

'You can cook?' She didn't try to hide her astonishment.

When he smiled her body's demands changed to hunger of a different sort. 'Of course I can cook,' he said calmly, opening the door into a room that turned out to be a kitchen.

Not just any old kitchen, either; this one was a chef's dream. He stood back to let her through, the courtesy so automatic it meant nothing.

'And I suppose you can climb mountains without oxygen and fight grizzly bears with your bare hands?' she scoffed, but she went ahead of him.

'No, I only tackle lions bare-handed. For grizzly bears I carry a knife between my teeth,' he said cheerfully.

Paige laughed spontaneously. After a swift, heart-shivering smile, he set about grilling bacon. Paige watched his efficient handling of kitchen tools with something like wonder.

She'd become accustomed to thinking of him as the man who sparked her hormones into a sexual frenzy—and as Juliette's husband. Forbidden fruit, in other words. His relationship with Lauren Porter had reinforced her view of him as a predator whose only interest outside business was sexual intrigue.

The man deftly cooking her breakfast bore no resemblance to the bogeyman she'd manufactured. And that made him more risky, because she could despise a sexual predator.

An hour later Paige got out of the car and said pleasantly, 'Thank you for breakfast. It was delicious.'

He glanced at the thin gold watch on his tanned wrist. 'I'll see you at nine.'

With a scintillating, seething glance she spluttered, 'That's ridiculous. I can't organise everything in such a short time.'

'In two hours, then,' he said inexorably, concealing his keen scrutiny with a veil of long lashes.

Used like that, they were weapons. Fighting their effect, she said stiffly, 'I can't promise anything.'

He smiled and said, 'At ten o'clock, Paige. Don't worry, I'll take care of everything.'

Watching Marc taking care of everything was an education in raw power.

Standing at the window, Sherry watched his car leave the car park and said in a stunned voice, 'Whew! Talk about dynamite. I can see how he got to be a zillionaire!' She looked self-consciously at Paige. 'I'm sorry you disapprove of him paying for me to stay home with Brodie.'

Paige continued firing clothes into the only case she possessed—a pack Lloyd had given her one Christmas. 'I don't disapprove,' she said lightly. 'It's got nothing to do with me. But won't your boss object?'

Looking slightly smug, and rather too self-conscious, Sherry shook her head. 'No. I know I shouldn't have taken Marc's money, but he's not going to miss it.'

It wasn't a question, but Paige answered it. 'No, of course not.' She added more clothes and her sponge bag, wishing with futile foolishness that she had some outfit that didn't proclaim its provenance—a mail-order catalogue. 'I hate surprises! I wish you hadn't told him where I was this morning.'

Sherry flushed and patted Brodie's back. 'He's not the sort of man you refuse,' she said a little guiltily.

'I know. Don't take any notice of me—I'm just angry at being more or less railroaded into this.'

'Are you sure it's a good idea?'

'No,' Paige said on a sigh. 'But—well, if Juliette wanted me to go to Arohanui to pick up her bequest, I feel I'd be letting her down if I didn't.' She tucked a pair of socks into her sandshoes and zipped up the pack. 'That will have to do.'

In the sitting room, Sherry sat down on the sofa and smiled at her son. He lifted a small arm and waved it around, cooing as his mother kissed his face.

'How come you were such great friends with his wife?' she asked. 'This dude of yours is seriously loaded; that sort marry their own kind. And usually they make friends with their own kind.'

'He's not my dude!' Paige filled the new kettle. Above the sound of running water, she said, 'Juliette and I lived next door to each other in Wellington. She was five years older, but she adored kids—she used to call me her pretty little sister, although she was the pretty one. When they moved I cried so much that she promised me I could be her bridesmaid. At eleven that's a big deal.'

Sherry looked intrigued. 'You're right. And she followed through?'

'Yes, with a week in Paris and the most gorgeous dress.'

And Marc's locket.

Sherry said drily, 'So Juliette was loaded too?'

'I never thought of it, but her family must have been. Her father was in the diplomatic service.'

'She sounds nice.'

'She was great—kind and fun. She kept in touch even after she was married.' Heat stung Paige's cheeks as she poured boiling water into the mugs.

'And then she got killed,' Sherry said sympathetically. 'That's tough.'

What was tougher was that for Marc the marriage had been a sham, a marriage of convenience entered into because he'd needed a suitable wife.

'Yes.' Frowning, Paige looked around. 'Now, are you sure you'll be OK?'

'We'll be fine,' Sherry repeated patiently. 'How did you get on with the dogs?'

'Mrs Greig grumbled, but the high school boy next door will do them until I come back.' She carried the two mugs of coffee across and sat down on a chair.

Sherry put Brodie down on the sofa to kick. 'You can't get out of this, so you might as well treat it like a mini-holiday,' she said, looking up from rapt admiration of his chubby legs. 'Heaven knows, you could do with it. You've had a rotten spin in the last year. It'll be warmer up in the Bay of Islands—see if you can get a little bit of tan.'

Paige looked up as a car drew up outside and Marc got out. 'Time to go,' she muttered, her heart jumping.

Sherry picked Brodie up and turned to scrutinise Marc. 'Oh, boy, he really is something,' she said softly. 'You be careful, Paige.'

Skin tightening, Paige went across and opened the door.

'Ready?' Marc asked.

'Yes.'

She stood back to let him in, and Paige wasn't surprised when Sherry, dazzled out of her usual cynicism where men were concerned, proudly handed the baby over to him.

Marc cradled him with confidence, smiling into the little face. For once the baby didn't deliver the usual roar he kept for strangers. Solemn-faced, he stared up at Marc, before producing a one-sided smile and clenching his fists in an energetic fashion.

'I think he knows me,' Marc said, smiling with immense charm.

Clearly dazzled, Brodie lifted an arm and waved it vaguely above his head while he produced soft gurgles.

Sherry nodded briskly and took the baby back. 'Looks

like it. Before you go, I'd better have an address and a phone number—just in case I need to contact you, Paige.'

'I'll give you my card.' Marc pulled a sleek wallet from his pocket and took out a card, scribbled on the back and handed it to Sherry.

She made no bones about reading it. 'Arohanui Island. Where's that?'

While Marc told her, Paige watched the corners of his mouth tuck in as he fought a smile. Of course he knew what Sherry was doing—her implied warning wasn't very subtle.

Sherry nodded, and, being a loyal daughter of the dry province of Hawke Bay, said, 'It rains a lot up there, I hear.'

'Not all the time,' Marc said with another dizzying smile. He stowed his wallet back in his pocket and looked across at Paige, a silent spectator. 'We should be going. The plane's waiting.'

He meant that quite literally. Half an hour later they were heading north in a chartered plane big enough to take ten or so people. Normally Paige would have enjoyed admiring New Zealand's wild central plateau, with its three snow-covered volcanoes marching southwards from Lake Taupo—its serene blue-grey waters the biggest crater of all—but there was nothing normal about the luxurious little plane or the trip.

She picked up a fashion magazine from the several the steward had presented to her after she'd refused his offer of champagne. The cover featured in loving and explicit detail a stunning red-headed woman clad in a swathe of silk and ostrich feathers; she appeared to be making love to a classical pillar.

Paige put the magazine down.

From the corner of her eye she could see Marc's hand

across the aisle as he sorted papers. They were beautiful—long-fingered and strong, competently shuffling the documents. What would they feel like—?

Don't go there! Now that she was actually on her way to his island she wondered how on earth she'd made such a decision. He must have bewitched her.

No, she'd let herself be overborne by his stronger will, and by a need to give Juliette whatever she had wanted with this odd request.

Why had she made it? And why ask that Marc wait so long after her death before contacting Paige? It didn't make sense.

She glanced sideways again, this time lifting her eyes to his face. He was now absorbed in reading one of the documents, his profile an autocratic harmony of lines and angles, but beneath the veneer of smoothly civilised power pulsed a dark arrogance, an uncompromising force of will that made her shiver inside.

He'd be a formidable enemy.

Dragging her eyes free, Paige leaned back and watched cloud shadows chase themselves over the green, green countryside beneath, Sherry's last words echoing in her mind.

As Marc had carried Paige's bag out to his car, her flatmate had muttered, 'Standing directly between you is like walking into a furnace.' She watched Marc close the boot of the car. 'I bet he's good,' she said, and smiled reminiscently. 'Be careful, Paige. But why don't you have some fun for once?'

Fun?

Paige stole another glance at the man reading papers with efficient speed. Her stomach clamped on a spasm of roiling sensation, sweet and strong and potent.

It wouldn't be fun. He might make love like a dark angel, but she stood to lose her heart if she—

Her mind closed down. She was *not* falling in love with him. Glaring at the hands in her lap, she forcibly reminded herself that he'd married Juliette for convenience, and the equally convenient Lauren Porter was still in the picture.

OK, so she felt something for him, but it certainly wasn't love. Lust, Marc had called it, and quoted Shakespeare with such contempt that she still felt cold when she thought of his voice, detached and brutally uncompromising, as he'd let her know exactly what he thought of this disruptive chemistry between them.

CHAPTER FIVE

SHE woke to hands at her waist and a darkly masculine voice forcing its way through compelling, X-rated dreams.

When she forced her lashes up Marc's tanned face swam into vision—too close, the hard features intent and purposeful. Her heart slammed into her throat as her dazed eyes met the burning blue of his. He was crouched in front of her, broad shoulders blocking out the aircraft cabin.

'What—?' she stammered, still fighting sleep and the corroding pleasure of his nearness. 'What is it? Are we there?'

'Not quite.'

His voice sounded guttural even to his own ears, and he took in a deep breath, watching her pupils dilate and darkness swamp the green-gold fire in an involuntary signal— one his body recognised and responded to with helpless, instant hunger that consigned caution to the rubbish bin. Every cell reacted with violent appreciation to her provocative, heavy-lidded gaze and the soft lips slightly parted in unconscious seduction.

'What are you doing?' Although the words emerged with a crisp bite he noted their husky, sensuous undertone.

'We'll be landing soon,' he said roughly. 'The seatbelt warning is on. I tried to fasten yours without waking you.'

Yet his hands refused to move, curving almost possessively against her midriff, just below her soft breasts. A feral, sensual heat set fire to his will power.

He knew love was a heartless cardsharp of an emotion, something he neither offered nor promised. Nevertheless he'd always made sure that his lovers—and his wife—understood that he liked and respected them.

And then the night before his wedding he'd looked into Paige's gold-green eyes and wanted her with a merciless craving. He despised men who used women; it had struck at some hidden vulnerability when he'd discovered that one glance from a girl he'd just met—a girl still at high school!—stripped back his controlled assurance to expose raw arousal.

It was like being taken over by an alien. Resentment couldn't kill it—didn't even dampen it. And neither had long years of denial.

When she moved her hands to cover his, and said in a lazy, throaty voice, 'I'll do it,' an odd sideways sensation, as though the world had shifted beneath his feet, catapulted him into unknown territory.

Her eyes trapped him in a smouldering snare and the touch of her hands sent forbidden messages straight to his brain and his loins. He'd never experienced hunger like this before, so intense it rolled over him like lava—dangerous, beautiful, lethally destructive.

In one lethal movement he snapped the ends of her seatbelt together and stood up, towering over her in deliberate intimidation.

'All right?' he asked, unable to drag his unwilling gaze from the pulse that jumped in her slender throat.

'Yes.' She flushed and looked away, straightening her shoulders with obvious effort. 'Sorry, it always takes me a while to wake up.'

Disgusted by his lack of control, Marc sat down quickly, before his body could betray him further. Fiercely disciplining his hands, he latched his own seatbelt across his flat stomach and fixed his eyes on the scene through the window, watching the panorama of sea and sky tilt below them.

It was no use; the loveliness outside faded as his mind supplied images of how Paige would look in his bed after a night spent making love, and how sensually, exquisitely magical it would be to wake her slowly...

God! If merely touching her could summon erotic fantasies, he should have stayed overseas and let his office organise this trip to Arohanui.

So why hadn't he?

The embarrassing answer sat beside him, her head turned away so that a dark honey-coloured swathe of hair hid her face. Although they weren't touching he could feel her closeness, smell the faint natural perfume of her skin, and see her hands from the corner of his eye. They lay loosely clasped in her lap, yet he sensed a tension to match his own.

She had long, competent fingers, and his treacherous mind supplied another sizzling picture of those hands on his skin, pale gold against bronze...

Perhaps, he thought coldly, he should follow this through and see where it took them both. It was nothing more than sexual chemistry, but when he was with her he felt—he felt like a lesser man, he warned himself with merciless honesty. Paige had power over him, power he refused to yield to her, because once she knew she possessed it she might be able to possess him.

In spite of that he wanted her, and he was experienced enough to read desire in a woman. So, why not accept what she unconsciously offered?

Because it *was* unconscious, and he didn't take advantage of innocents.

Yet how many women of her age were as inexperienced as she seemed to be? Perhaps it was a ruse...

Dressed properly, pampered and groomed, she'd make a stunning mistress. It would be a partnership of equals—she'd see the world, have some fun, learn a lot, and when he'd got her out of his system he'd make sure she never had to work again if she didn't want to.

Surely that would be better than the life she was leading now?

'Where do we land?' she asked, her voice tight and remote, as composed as the face she turned towards him.

He raked her with a hard gaze, noted the colour rising through her silky golden skin. She swallowed and her tongue stole out to moisten her parted lips. Yes, she wanted him.

Temptation riding him hard, he said, 'Kerikeri. It's the nearest commercial airport to the Bay.'

Paige turned back to watching the sea spin beneath the plane, and dragged a juddering breath into painful lungs. Every instinct shrieked a warning—too late. Because in the mindless, temporary no-man's land between sleep and awakening she'd betrayed herself.

Marc had recognised her response as sexual excitement. She'd seen disgust ice his eyes and freeze his face.

Juliette had told her about the women who chased him, the open lures they'd tossed in his way, the subterfuges they'd used to try and coax him into their beds. And she'd told her about his contempt for them.

Pride stiffened Paige's shoulders, clenched her jaw. So he assumed she was just like them—sexually available, light-heartedly promiscuous. Her soft lips tightened. He'd probably laugh if he knew she had never made love. Not that he'd ever find out.

From now on she'd be as aloof as he was.

Jaw jutting, she stared blindly through the window, her

self-possession evaporating when his voice—too close—sounded above the roar of the engines.

A subtly abrasive note threading each word, he said, 'We're turning over the Bay of Islands. You should be able to see Arohanui Island.' He leaned forward and pointed across her. 'There.'

Tensely aware that he took great care not to touch her, Paige followed his finger.

Heart-shaped, mysterious, his island lay in a glinting, swirling sea the colour of a blue-green opal. Around it more scraps of land dotted a huge bay, some sombre with native bush, others a bright, sharp green. She blinked at beaches so bright they made her think of diamond dust, and others an elusive shade that reminded her of the champagne she'd drunk at his wedding—pale and soft with a tawny glow.

'Is it called Arohanui because of its shape? The name means great love, doesn't it?' she asked.

Shocked by the sultry, too intimate tone of her voice, she discreetly cleared her throat and kept her eyes fixed on the island.

'Yes. But its name refers to an old Maori legend about doomed lovers, not its shape,' he said drily. 'It was called that long before the first Corbett settled here.'

'It's very beautiful.' She cast around for something else to say, falling back on a banal comment. 'I've seen photographs, of course, but I didn't realise how many islands there are in the Bay.'

'Over a hundred and fifty, I'm told. It depends on exactly what you call an island. Haven't you been here before?'

'Not that I know of. When I was a kid we used to go to Fiji and the Gold Coast in Australia.' Her reminiscent smile faded. 'And when I was eleven my mother took me to Disneyland in California.'

It had been an almost perfect holiday, spoiled only because her father hadn't gone with them. He hadn't been at home when they'd arrived back, either; while they'd been away he'd moved in with his secretary, taking holidays and colour and laughter with him.

'My father was born on the island,' Marc told her. 'He loved it. My mother thinks it a little unsophisticated. She prefers her scenic beauty well tamed and controlled.'

Paige remembered his mother well—a worldly woman with the effortless, casual elegance of a daughter of France. She and Juliette had got on well.

His face hardened into cold, bleak bronze. 'She says she always knew that the island would claim him. He went out to see if he could rescue a boatload of idiots who took off for a day's fishing without checking the forecast or bothering about life-jackets, radio or flares. They all died.'

Paige made a shocked noise. 'I'm so sorry.'

He shrugged. 'He enjoyed risky enterprises. He'd rather have gone down like that than dwindle into old age.'

Chilled, Paige looked into cold, crystalline eyes. Marc, she realised, didn't think like that; he was too responsible to indulge in grand gestures for the adrenaline rush.

For some obscure reason this insight comforted her. She turned back and stared resolutely down. Trees crowned the intricate tucks and folds of Arohanui, but from the air she could see the red-brown shape of a roof surrounded by large gardens. It must have rained recently, because the island gleamed like polished greenstone.

'It looks mysterious, enchanted,' she said softly. 'A place removed from time and space where everyday rules might be suspended.'

'That's the lure of islands. They offer a hint of the forbidden, the exotic, a dangerous beauty.'

His almost indifferent words echoed in her mind like a challenge.

Don't even consider it! Paige commanded, quashing a piercing excitement to fix her attention solely on the island that slipped away beneath the aircraft wing, swift and inevitable as the remnants of a lovely dream.

'I thought you preferred Paris,' she said.

'I love Paris. I like London and New York too. But Arohanui has always been my home.'

She had to stop herself from turning to look at him. Juliette had complained of boredom and the lack of sophisticated entertainment on Arohanui, and after the first year of their marriage Marc had visited it alone.

Paige fixed her eyes on the view and concentrated on reminding herself that, like her father, Marc had been unfaithful to his wife.

It didn't work. She couldn't think of anything else but the man beside her. Barely discernible, how did his natural scent make such an impact, kicking her heart into a gallop and drying her mouth?

Sex, she told herself robustly. Think pheromones and moths dying dramatically in candle flames. If you give in to it, you'll be betraying your friendship with Juliette.

And you might fall in love with him...

Not likely, she scoffed. Oh, there must be some men who could love selflessly, but she'd seen precious few of them. Betrayed love had driven her mother into the acute depression that had ruined her life; Sherry's husband had promised her a love for all eternity, then robbed her and abandoned her when she'd told him of her pregnancy. Even Marc's mother had been left alone and forlorn after her husband's gallant, foolhardy death.

Paige jutted her jaw and watched a couple of small seaside towns race beneath the wings; as long as she stayed independent, no one could hurt her.

'The villages are Paihia and Russell,' Marc said in a manner that hinted at mockery—and not the pleasantly teasing kind, either. 'Holiday towns, both of them, although Russell has some interesting old buildings. We'll be coming in over Kerikeri any minute—you'll see orchards and vineyards.'

Almost immediately a formal chequerboard landscape divided by hedges began to slip by; kicked by swift panic, Paige closed her eyes and gulped, wondering what the hell she was doing here.

Warmth enclosed her hand as Marc took it. 'It's all right,' he said, his voice deep and calm. 'Relax, we're just coming in to land.'

Feeling unutterably stupid, she let her hand lie in the warmth of his, wondering how so comforting a grip could also send charges of excitement up her arm to shut down her brain. She forced her eyes open as the plane levelled off over farmlands.

'Kerikeri Airport,' Marc said calmly, nodding towards a small cluster of buildings. 'We transfer to the helicopter here.' He dropped her hand to indicate a machine parked off the runway.

Paige swallowed. Marc was rich; she'd always known that. The locket he'd given her had been valued at an extraordinary price because of its workmanship and the quality of the diamond. He had houses scattered over the globe and, because he liked his privacy, he'd bought several islands.

Even his clothes, casual though they were, breathed an aura of wealth.

But this offhand use of chartered planes brought home to her just how much money—and power—he had.

Her mind raced, chanting, *You shouldn't have come, you shouldn't have come.*

She looked down at her faded jeans. He was a different species, she told herself with a hard practicality that somehow didn't ring true. You're only here to pick up Juliette's legacy. Tomorrow he's going back to his world and after a pleasant, uneventful week in beautiful surroundings you'll go back to yours, back to real life.

And you'll never see him again.

The sombre words emptied out her heart and rang through the furthest reach of her brain.

As the engines changed in pitch and the plane slowed she asked something that had been niggling in the back of her mind since she'd looked up to see him come towards her and the dogs. 'How did you know where I was this morning? Sherry said she could only give you general directions; I don't always go to the same place with the dogs.'

He paused, before telling her calmly, 'I had you checked out. My private detective told me you walked the dogs every week day and that you kept to a regular routine between parks and the beach.'

Her temper flashed. Staring straight ahead, she said rigidly, 'That is completely outrageous.'

'Just another perk of being obscenely rich,' he said blandly. 'It wouldn't have been necessary if you'd been a bit more forthcoming instead of clamming up and hissing every time I tried to find out anything.' He sounded cool, even mildly amused.

The plane touched down with a slight bump and taxied towards the buildings. As Paige sat fuming he ended with a caustic note, 'And I'm sure nothing would have persuaded you to tell me that you'd been sacked because you wouldn't sleep with your boss.'

'How did you find—?' Bright coins of colour standing out on her cheeks, she grated, 'Don't you dare say I've just told you.'

'All right, then, I won't,' he said obligingly. 'It wouldn't be true. I'll bet he wondered what the hell had bitten him when he tried to force you into bed.'

'He didn't get the chance,' she said with cutting disdain. 'The first time he groped me I told him I'd complain of harassment if he ever tried it again.' Colour touched her skin. For weeks she'd felt dirty, as though the man's touch had contaminated her.

'So he sacked you?'

A swift glance revealed a dangerous razor-edge of light in the depths of his eyes. Shaken, Paige looked away to marshal her thoughts. 'I was made redundant. Last hired, first off. And it was a bad year for farmers so the firm didn't have enough work for me... Actually, I was glad to go.'

Although if she'd known how difficult it was going to be to get another job she might have fought to stay, in spite of the creep.

Marc said in a voice that contradicted his searching gaze, 'He's spread it around the city that you're a predatory female who backs demands for an increase in wages with threats.'

Angry and bewildered, she stared at him. 'Threats? Threats of *what*?'

'According to him, you said that if you didn't get a rise you'd accuse him of sexual harassment.' He spoke in a detached, judicial tone that lifted the hairs on the back of her neck.

The plane slowed, easing to a stop. Her voice molten,

Paige said, 'So *that's* why I've had no luck finding a new job. I should have put his pot on.'

'Why didn't you? You weren't the first woman he'd tried it on with, and you must have known he'd do it again. Sleazes like him always do.'

Trust him to unerringly pinpoint the one thing that still worried her. She said defensively, 'It was my word against his. He's a well-known personality in Napier; why would anyone believe me? How did your private detective find out?'

'By asking questions of a couple of women who'd left that office suddenly. One of them was your predecessor.' The plane rolled smoothly to a stop. Marc got to his feet and said, 'It doesn't matter, anyway.'

And when she looked up in disgust he gave her a cold, merciless smile that jetted an icy touch the length of her spine. 'His firm now knows exactly what's been happening. He's got one chance to keep his job, and that's to keep his hands, his innuendoes and everything else to himself. He's also been—persuaded—to stop spreading slander about you. I don't think you'll have any trouble getting a similar position when you go back.'

Paige's jaw dropped, but the pilot's voice over the intercom stopped the hot words tumbling from her lips.

'Here we are in lovely sub-tropical Kerikeri,' he announced, 'gateway to the Bay of Islands. Hope you had a good flight.'

Pasting a jaunty smile on her lips, Paige said, 'Coincidence is a funny thing. Just think, if I hadn't come down the stairs of the hotel at the exact moment you turned around, you'd never have known that I lived in Napier.'

Marc's eyes were cool and opaque, as unreadable as the expression on his gorgeous face. 'New Zealand's not that big—I'd have found you.' He stood back to let her out into the aisle.

Something about his tone made her deeply uneasy. Trying to ignore the crawling tension between her shoulderblades, she got up.

The steward emerged to open the door, nodding respectfully as they stepped out into sultry sunlight and air that even the taint of aviation fuel couldn't sully.

Refusing to look at Marc, Paige decided there was a difference about the atmosphere up here—somehow the countryside glowed, softer yet more vivid than the crisp clarity she was used to. The grass radiated green light around them as they walked across to the helicopter where another pilot waited.

Not that he was needed. The helicopter belonged to Marc, and it was he who flew them to the island, landing the chopper precisely on a hard pad several hundred metres from the homestead.

The big house sprawled in magnificent gardens beside a half-moon of beach; as they'd flown down Paige had noted a grass tennis court and a swimming pool, and what appeared to be a large two-masted yacht in the bay, anchored beside a motor cruiser.

Rich man's paradise, she thought, struggling for balance and common sense, trying not to be overwhelmed. She knew Marc worked hard; Juliette had told her about his frequent absences and the long hours spent at his desk. But it didn't seem fair that Sherry had to display her body to earn enough for a place of her own when Marc had all this—and it was just one of his residences!

The rotors died, and she realised Marc was turning around. Into the sudden silence he said formally, 'Welcome to my home.'

'Thank you,' Paige said, enmeshed in an odd, swift shyness, because it seemed as though he was making some sort of statement.

Which was ridiculous. No doubt the formal welcome had been just a bit of old-world courtesy.

Marc was disloyal, a breaker of vows. Quite possibly the executive-cum-mistress whose existence had shattered Juliette's life was already in residence, honing her cutting English accents for more put-downs.

The house seemed to grow in size as they walked through the garden towards it. Clinging desperately to her composure, Paige refused to gawk like a sightseer—although that was difficult once they were inside.

Not that the house was decorated in incongruous splendour. For all its size it breathed a warm, casual sophistication that made her feel instantly at home. After being introduced to the housekeeper, a middle-aged woman called Rose Oliver, Paige was ushered by her to a bedroom overlooking the bay.

Paige eyed the vast bed, its white calico spread tucked into a box frame of dark, warmly coloured wood. White walls breathed understated elegance; one displayed a magnificent kimono in black and cinnamon and a blue almost the same intense hue as Marc's eyes, and on the wall behind the bedhead a triptych glowed like a jewel in the cool, beautiful room—a spare, exquisitely painted Japanese scene of mountains and river.

Apart from a terracotta pot holding a flourishing banana tree there were no other decorations, although the wall of stained wood shutters onto a terrace gave the room texture and pattern.

'The wardrobes are in here,' the housekeeper said, gesturing towards a door in the wall. 'Would you like me to unpack for you?'

'No, thank you.' Paige tried to sound at ease. The last

thing she wanted was to let someone who probably regularly ministered to heiresses see her clothes.

After showing her the bathroom, Mrs Oliver said, 'I'm sure you'd like a shower. I'll call for you in about an hour, shall I? If there's anything you need, don't hesitate to ring.' She pointed to a telephone tucked into a shelf below the headboard. 'The numbers are on the set.'

She smiled and left the room.

All very polite and friendly, Paige thought as she headed into the large tiled bathroom. A huge shower covered an indecent amount of the floor, and an even larger spa bath took up another corner. Sunlight shimmered through palm fronds and dark shutters onto creamy marble and gleaming glass.

A delicious perfume led her to the soap; she lifted the cake and smelt it, then set it down again with a firm, set smile. Her own brand was fine. It was stupid, but if she used the soap that Marc's money had provided she'd feel she'd been bought.

As she wallowed in hot water from four directions, she wondered if anyone quite so poverty stricken had ever been a guest in Marc's house before.

Who cared? 'Enjoy it while you can,' she told her reflection defiantly.

Her scruples, if scruples were what they were, didn't extend to not using the hairdryer, also bought with his money!

She got into a pair of olive-green trousers before tucking in her bittersweet red shirt. A final glance in the mirror revealed that the trousers hung a little loosely on her hips. Frowning, she pulled out the shirt to cover them.

Only just ready when someone knocked on the door—according to her watch, twenty minutes early—she opened it. Her smile set when she saw who waited outside.

CHAPTER SIX

LIKE her, Marc had changed. In trousers that skimmed his strongly muscled thighs and a sports shirt one shade paler than his eyes he looked big and unyielding—and forbiddingly attractive.

Paige's heart kicked into a gallop, and she had to swallow hard to dislodge her breath from its sticking place in her throat.

'Oh—I thought you were Mrs Oliver—the housekeeper,' she blurted, only just saving herself from stammering.

Narrowed, steely eyes examined her face. 'Would you like a look around before lunch?'

'Thank you.' She wanted to ask him about Juliette's legacy, but it seemed crass and greedy. Instead she walked sedately beside him down the wide hall and out onto a terrace running along the front of the house.

She had to admit that Marc was an excellent host. With impeccable courtesy he showed her the garden between the house and the beach, a sub-tropical fantasy that fascinated her with its skilful mingling of colour and form and scent.

On the way back towards the house they passed the tennis court, and he asked if she played.

'I used to,' she said. 'But not for a while.'

'Perhaps we could have a game some time.'

Which meant never, of course. 'Perhaps,' she said noncommittally. She turned away and looked out over the bay. 'Are those boats—the yacht and the cruiser—yours?'

'Yes. Do you like sailing?'

'I loved it when I was a kid,' she told him, adding, 'My father had a yacht.'

He frowned. 'I'll take you out one day.'

Like the suggestion of tennis, she knew he didn't mean it. What was the sense of all this? Tomorrow he'd be gone.

He was just being polite, as though she was a real guest here, not someone he'd been obliged to host by his dead wife's will—the wife he'd betrayed.

Abruptly she asked, 'Where is Juliette's box?'

Thick black lashes concealed his eyes for a second, then lifted to reveal intensely blue depths, unreadable and enigmatic. 'I'll have it sent to your room.'

In crackling silence, they walked up the steps to the wide terrace.

'It's a wonderful house,' Paige said woodenly. 'So warm and sunny, yet the eaves must keep out the summer sun. And the garden is magical!'

Marc watched her face, saw something like wistfulness there, and silently summoned a raw French oath at the wave of protectiveness he felt. It had to be because she was Juliette's friend. And because she'd had a rotten time with that bastard she'd worked for. As well, she hadn't entirely recovered from the flu.

A man who prided himself on facing the truth without flinching, he let the comforting lies lodge in his brain for a betraying moment, until cold anger banished them.

Yes, he felt some responsibility for Juliette's friend, because she was in trouble. But this strange need to care for her was something he'd never experienced before.

He was gentle with women because they were smaller and more fragile, although he respected their different kind of strength and their endurance when many men gave up.

And he didn't prey on the weak; he chose only those sophisticated enough to look after themselves.

Even Juliette, he thought with a brief, hard smile, young as she'd been, had known exactly what she wanted.

But Paige got to him; he resented the fact that any offer of help would be flung back in his teeth. Determination shone from her face, from the set of her shoulders and the resolute line of her soft, tantalising mouth.

Although he admired her for it, he wanted to smash that challenging pride into shards and make her totally, completely dependent on him.

He'd never felt like that before.

Brusquely he said, 'Lunch must be ready.'

It was served at a table on the terrace, under the benign and hopeful gaze of a golden retriever called Fancy, each mouthful of delicious food accompanied by enthusiastic, fearless chattering from a pair of fantails, tiny birds that swooped through the warm air as they sought unseen insects.

Desperate to subdue the rising tension, Paige said brightly, 'They're such friendly little birds, aren't they? It's difficult to think of them as mighty hunters.'

Marc's smile hardened. 'Like them, we're all hunters,' he said, 'and we're all prey.'

Shocked, she lifted her lashes. He was watching her with half-closed eyes, and as little rills of flame ran wild through her body he lowered his gaze to her mouth.

Deliberately intimate, blatant as a kiss, the brief glance burned through her defences. Colour flamed into her skin and she couldn't think of anything to say—she who had been extremely vocal when her sleazy employer had tried to hit on her!

Finally she managed, 'That's an interesting perspective on personal relationships.'

With a slight Gallic shrug he stated inflexibly, 'It's the truth. Look at your flatmate.'

'Sherry?' She bristled. 'She's not a victim and she's certainly not—'

'She wants money from the men who watch her strip.' His coolly dispassionate voice doused her spurt of temper. 'The more provocative her routine—the more she promises with each gesture and movement—the more money she makes. But I doubt if she follows through on it.'

'She doesn't,' Paige snapped. 'She's a dancer.'

'So it's a coldly commercial transaction—she encourages her customers to fantasise about her without giving them any warmth or tenderness or respect.'

Paige blinked and cast a swift glance at his angular features. It seemed an odd thing for a man who kept a mistress to say. How much warmth or tenderness or respect had he given Juliette? She could glean nothing from his face beyond a quizzical gleam in the blue eyes.

She said stiffly, 'She's doing it for Brodie's sake. As for warmth and tenderness and so on, I don't imagine many of the men who watch her dance go to the club for that.'

'Your loyalty is praiseworthy,' he drawled, not hiding the mockery in his tone. 'So why aren't *you* stripping for a living? She's earning more than you are.'

Her appetite vanishing, Paige put down her fork and looked him straight in the eye. 'Because I can do other things, and I don't have a child to plan for,' she stated coldly. 'Sherry grew up in a horrifying family situation and ended up on the streets when she was only fourteen. She got herself off them by sheer guts, then she married, sure it was going to last for ever. When she told her husband she was pregnant with Brodie he scarpered off to Australia, leaving a pile of debts he'd run up in her name. She doesn't enjoy working as a stripper, but her long-term plan is to make enough money to get out and give Brodie a decent life.'

'That makes her prey,' he said calmly, and changed the subject with an insulting blandness. 'Eat up—it's a long time since breakfast, and you didn't have anything on the flight, so you must be hungry.'

He was right. Although Paige's mouth set mutinously, she was hungry, and while she cleared her plate of a delicious salad that combined beans and strawberries Marc told her Arohanui's ancient legend of two Maori lovers who laid down their lives for each other.

Lulled by sunshine and a deep, highly suspect pleasure, Paige clung to her common sense by sheer exercise of will. When he'd finished she said lightly, 'How very romantic and tragic—*Romeo and Juliet*, South Pacific-style.'

His answering smile was smoothly mocking. 'And you don't believe a word of it.'

'If it happened, I'll bet they were very young.'

'Meaning that only the young and naïve consider love worth dying for?' He leaned back in his chair, long fingers curved around the stem of his wine glass, those thick lashes hiding his thoughts. 'You could be right.'

Uneasily aware that for all his relaxed grace he was focused intently on her, she opened her mouth to answer, but was forestalled when his brilliant gaze took her prisoner.

'How old are you? Twenty-three? From my perspective that's pretty young,' he finished on a note of amusement.

Heat washed through her in a smooth, feral response, shutting down her mind until the dog sat up to snap at a fly and the familiar, tiny sound dragged her back to reality.

Paige looked away and said stiffly, 'If it's cynical to believe that love is a much overrated emotion, then I suppose I must be cynical.'

His brows rose above glinting, metallic eyes, but he said mildly, 'I agree entirely with you that love is a much over-rated emotion.'

Well, she'd known that—so why did her heart contract painfully? 'How astonishing! We have something in common,' she flashed, then bit her lip.

He nodded. 'My parents supposedly loved each other, but all I remember of them was the sound of their quarrels. And their silences.'

Paige looked down. A gleam of sunlight probed a knife-blade with metallic glitter. 'My parents didn't quarrel. My mother told me that she'd had no idea—she thought they had a wonderful marriage until we arrived back from Disneyland to find my father living with his secretary. I think that was why she never got over it.'

The moment the words were said she wished them back; wincing internally, she braced herself for his response.

Sunlight collected in mahogany pools in his hair as he looked down at her. 'That must have been a difficult time.'

'As I suppose you know, there's no easy way to deal with marriage disasters. I managed,' she said curtly, accepting a cup of coffee from him.

'But your mother didn't.'

Shocked, she looked up into eyes that were steady and sympathetic. 'Your private detective has been busy.'

'Drink up,' he said, not disturbed by her bitterness. 'After you've finished your coffee, why don't you rest for an hour or so?'

In her bedroom, Paige decided ironically that he was good; he'd managed to cloak a desire to get rid of her with common courtesy. She'd even believed him—until she was free of his overpowering magnetism.

Stretching out on the daybed, she tried emptying her mind, but it kept replaying that enigmatic conversation over the table. She'd said too much, revealed more of herself than was wise. It gave Marc an advantage, because all she knew of him was that he had a particularly continental way of running his sex-life.

Well, no, now she knew that his parents' marriage had been unhappy. Had he intended to tell her? He was so controlled a man that his oddly intimate disclosure had to be deliberate.

When she found herself daydreaming of other intimate disclosures—sexy, basic, urgent fantasies that smoked through her brain in a drugging miasma—she leapt to her feet and paced across the room to peer through the shutters into the sunlight, frowning ferociously as she reined in her vivid imagination.

Trying to be dispassionate and worldly, she decided that it was a pity she was still a virgin, at the mercy of her imagination when it came to men and sex! With even one lover tucked in her background she'd be more rational about Marc's elemental effect on her.

Feverish shivers chased each other down her spine. Looking like a lover from an erotic fantasy didn't make him some super-stud who'd automatically whisk her to the stars if he ever took her to bed.

First experience, she'd read, usually failed dismally to live up to expectations. Marc was dangerously attractive—and powerful and arrogantly confident—but he was only a man. He couldn't work miracles, and if she'd made love previously she'd have outgrown these romantic, overblown illusions of the perfect lover.

'Anyway, it's not going to happen,' she muttered, turning back to the daybed. An experienced man, Marc probably demanded all sorts of sexual expertise and techniques from his lovers.

She willed herself to think of more sober things, like

the fact that when she went back to Napier she might find herself a job…

Thanks to Marc.

Slowly, inevitably, as the island drowsed under the afternoon sun, sleep took over and her secret desires wound through her dreams.

She was smiling when a sharp noise forced her from Marc's arms, hurling her into the cold water splash of reality.

Dazed and disorientated, she tried to hide a yawn as she stumbled off the daybed and across the room, conscious only of the imperative knock as she opened the door.

Marc looked down into her bemused face, black brows drawn together, his beautiful mouth hardening.

'Are you all right?' he asked abruptly.

Colour swarmed up through her skin, heating it into acute sensitivity. Not only was her body aching with a hot, forbidden hunger, but her clothes were crumpled, her hair tangled around her face—and it seemed utterly elderly to sleep in the afternoon.

'I'm fine,' she croaked, adding with a brave attempt at poise, 'for someone who a moment ago was being chased by pirates.'

One pirate, actually.

And why had she said that? Marc's raised brow made her feel insignificant and stupid, yet she couldn't drag her eyes away from his face. Deep inside her something shattered into shards so fine she knew she'd never be able to put them together again. She suspected it was her precious independence. Every instinct shrilling an alarm, she took a step back from the door.

'Then it's just as well I woke you up,' he said promptly, but something had changed. A raw undertone deepened his voice and darkness swallowed some of the brilliance of his eyes.

'I—yes.' Her lips were dry, but she didn't dare lick them. 'I'll just wash my face.'

The words fell into a charged silence, one made even more significant by Marc's slight shrug. 'Of course,' he said non-committally. 'I'll be out on the terrace. I thought you might like to walk up the hill behind the house.'

Desperate to shatter the disturbing intimacy, Paige nodded. She needed violent activity to burn off the adrenaline that alerted every cell in her body; climbing a mountain would be ideal, but a walk should help.

'I won't be a moment,' she said, and stepped back, closing the door behind her.

When he turned that lethal male charm onto her she had to guard every response in case she fell into the oldest trap in the world—the sex trap. Paige washed her face and took a couple of deep, grounding breaths before going out to join him.

She stopped in the wide doorway onto the terrace, her heart picking up speed. Tall, darkly dominant against the light, he stood with his hands in his pockets and a broad shoulder leaning against one of the columns that held up the pergola. The dog Fancy sat beside him, following his gaze out to the gleaming sorcery of the ocean and the islands.

Because he had his back to her Paige could allow her eyes to appreciate the way the superbly tailored fabric strained over his lean hips and moulded the strong muscles in his thighs.

An odd, twisting sensation caught her by surprise, as did a swift pulse of heat in the pit of her stomach.

Paige set her teeth and moved out to join him, pointing

to a line of cloud bulging ominously over distant hills on the mainland. 'Is that rain on the way?'

His hands emerged from his pockets as he straightened up to cast a knowledgeable eye at the dark bar along the horizon. 'The wind's gone round to the south-west, so it's more than likely.' Frowning, he examined her with a swift, perceptive survey, then returned his attention to the distant hills. 'It's not travelling fast enough to worry us, and often clouds like that don't make it this far out in the Bay. Will you be warm enough?'

Too warm. In fact, she was heatedly, uncomfortably, *unbearably* aware of him.

And also aware that probably no other guest in his house had worn clothes as undistinguished as hers. Not that Marc gave any indication he'd noticed, but he'd have to be obtuse not to realise that her T-shirt and cotton trousers couldn't compare with the exquisite outfit of the woman who'd been with him that first day in Napier.

And he was far from obtuse.

'It's not cold,' she said, a shiver of alienation driving her to the edge of the terrace, where she pretended to scan the flamboyant combination of tropical and traditional garden forms.

After he'd left the island she'd spend some days storing this place in her memories. The plantswoman she longed to be relished the way fan palms set off native New Zealand shrubs and trees, and was excited by the exotic touch of upright cannas and bird of paradise flowers in electric blue and orange against the sprawling, extravagantly sombre splendour of two ancient pohutukawa trees.

She observed, 'I suppose if you live on an island you need to understand the weather.' And then flushed, remembering too late the circumstances of his father's tragic death.

'It's not so vital as it used to be; we have the latest gadgets for forecasting, and the locals are pretty good at reading the signs.' He gestured towards a path across the lawn. 'This way.'

As they set off, with the dog racing ahead, he added with an inflection that came too close to mockery, 'It's steep, so we should work off some of the tension of being inactive all day.'

The tension twisting along her nerves, Paige thought grimly, didn't come from inactivity.

The path led through a gate into a stand of huge, gnarled old pohutukawa trees, then struck off up a bush-clad hill. Paige liked the fact that apart from rock steps in the steepest pinches the track hadn't been formed, winding its way up beside a little stream that chattered musically over rocks. Nikau palms and the softer, feathery fronds of tree ferns crowded close in stately, graceful profusion, blending into the dark mass of bush.

'It smells deliciously fresh,' Paige said. Oh, wonderful—just be as banal as you can! Other women—the woman with him in Napier, for one—would have been able to entertain him with lively, witty conversation. 'And green, and somehow ancient,' she added defiantly, stepping from one rock to another across the creek as Fancy splashed gloriously through the water.

'It's never been cut over, so some of these trees are centuries old.' Marc was right behind her.

She concentrated fiercely on setting a cracking pace. Of course he kept up with her—and *he* wasn't breathless with exertion within ten minutes! Paige was grateful that he didn't try to speak, seemingly content to climb the slope in silence apart from an occasional command to the dog.

Sunlight stabbed golden shafts through the thick, scented canopy. 'Oh—look!' Paige breathed, slowing her pace and pointing, entranced by an arrow of light glowing like a halo around a small violet toadstool.

But the light vanished as though someone had yanked a shutter across, turning the green solitude into a murky gloom, still and threatening.

She said, 'Has that cloud—?'

'Quiet!'

Like him, she stopped, following his frowning gaze up into the sky, suddenly dark through the tangle of leaves. Above the short, soft sounds of her breathing she heard a bird cry out with shocking clarity in the tense silence. Fancy whined and pressed herself against Marc's legs.

'Thunder,' Marc said tersely, clearly angry with himself. 'I should have seen it coming.'

The distant mutter startled Paige, but not as much as the hand on her shoulder.

Exerting considerable pressure, he turned her and propelled her down the track. 'That squall is blowing in fast. We're almost at the top of the highest hill around, and under trees—perfect targets for lightning. Fancy, *come*!'

Another clap of thunder, nearer now, reinforced his warning. Fingers tightening on her shoulder, he gave her a little push, ordering curtly, 'Faster!'

Paige began to run, picking her way down the path as the thunder rumbled closer and closer and the light faded into a waiting, taut dimness. She could feel the turbulent, dangerous energy building within the clouds.

Although she skidded a couple of times she kept her balance. Marc could have easily outrun her, but he stayed a step ahead, positioning himself so that if she fell she'd land on him.

Always the protective male, she thought, trying to quench a warm glow in the most secret region of her heart. It meant nothing—a male hangover from prehistoric times when a man had to be ready to defend his woman against predators both animal and human.

He had no need to worry about wild animals in New Zealand, and she wasn't his woman, but she began to understand the seductive lure of masculine strength and power.

A strange exhilaration blossomed beneath her heart, expanding to fill her with bubbles of delight. Instinct warned her she'd always remember this mad dash down the hill through the moist gloom; time wouldn't overcome the steamy rich aroma of leaf-mould, or the sight of Fancy tearing down ahead, gold hair flying, ears lifting and falling.

And Marc, moving silently and powerfully, all controlled, huntsman's grace.

He glanced over his shoulder. 'OK?'

Oh, more than OK—foolishly, crazily exultant! 'Fine!'

Trying to curb this wild intoxication of the spirit, she began to count the intervals between the lightning that pulsed in staccato flashes through the trees and its accompanying thunder.

'We're lucky—the full force of the squall is going to miss the island,' Marc said into the waiting silence. 'Keep going—we're nearly there.'

But a few hundred metres from the garden he grabbed her hand and hauled her ruthlessly into a stand of graceful small trees, their sinuous branches holding up huge leaves that formed an umbrella.

'These will keep us reasonably dry,' he said.

She protested, 'We could make the house—'

'Not without soaking you—and this rain will be cold. It feels like hail.'

Sure enough, the temperature had dropped noticeably.

'I'm not made of sugar,' Paige said, but her heart wasn't in it.

Eyes glinting in the premature dusk, he surveyed her upturned face. 'Far from sugary,' he said in a detached, impersonal tone. 'Rain is one thing, but hail can kill.'

Although they couldn't see the rapidly approaching storm through the tree canopy, its presence was all around—borne on the wind that propelled its hissing advance towards them.

That cold breath flowed over Paige, rapidly banishing the heat from her headlong race down the hill. She clenched her teeth together, but couldn't stop a shiver. Marc pushed her behind him, sheltering her from the full onrush of the squall.

He said, 'Here it comes.'

Rain pounced, spattering noisily on the huge, glossy leaves before settling into a solid, heavy drumming that blocked out any thunder and turned twilight into darkness. A sudden gust lashed the trees, spattering huge drops over them. Marc stood foursquare onto the thrust of the storm, Fancy pressed against his legs.

Although cold, and a little damp around the edges, that suspicious euphoria still bubbled through Paige like the very best champagne. Groping for a steady place to anchor her emotions, she reminded herself of all the reasons she had to distrust this man.

Yet he'd put himself between her and the full force of the storm, and because of him her blood sang a primitive, taboo song while her body seethed with eager life.

She thought wildly that she'd remember this moment on her deathbed.

And, because that terrified her, she tried to push past him, saying hoarsely, 'I'm already wet—I might as well go on.'

He turned and grabbed her wrist, giving it a swift shake as he yanked her back. Harshly he snapped, 'Don't be an idiot. It could still hail. It will be over in a few minutes, so—'

The words fell into a silence that wasn't real, a silence conjured by pitiless awareness. I won't look up, she thought defiantly. I will not look up…

But she did, straight into the blue heart of fire, into eyes both penetrating and molten at the same time.

He said something she'd never learned in high school French and let her wrist go. Some unregenerate part of her realised that it took him a huge effort to release her, and gloated.

She didn't step back; she couldn't. As the thunder muttered and grumbled above them she said one word.

'That's the first time you've ever said my name.' His voice was harsh and deep and textured with hunger. 'Paige.'

Only one syllable, yet it was a caress, a note of raw need, a sensual promise.

But he waited, his eyes keen and measuring as they raked her face.

What was he doing? Demanding that she take the first step to surrender?

A stray raindrop plopped onto her lips, startling her into licking it off. He made a soft, feral sound that sent chills scudding the length of her spine, and the next moment she was being strained against his big, aroused body and he was kissing her, his mouth cool and controlled against hers—for a mini-second.

Until his steely discipline shattered into splinters and they kissed like long-separated lovers, as though they had kissed a thousand times before—as though after this there would be no other kiss, no other touch.

CHAPTER SEVEN

THE day her boss had tried to force her mouth open beneath his, Paige had efficiently backed away before scorching his ears with a contemptuous verbal assault.

Yet now, when Marc did the same thing, she opened to him gladly, linking her hands behind his back and dizzily surrendering to the desperate urgency that surged through her like fire in dry fern. More thunder hammered in her ears, her heart's insistent counterpoint to the tumult around them.

This, she realised as his mouth took hers again in fierce possession, was what she'd recognised in herself the first time she'd seen Marc—a wild hunger that knew no boundaries and suffered no restraints.

His arms tightened, bringing her against his hardening body. Every instinct of self-preservation shrieked at her to wrench free and race through the dying storm to the safety of the house.

But older, more basic instincts challenged her to stay, to find out what made Marc Corbett the only man with the power to smash down the conditioning of a lifetime.

And while she hovered between the promise of safety and the dazzling, embargoed beauty of danger, he kissed her just under the line of her jawbone, and one long-fingered hand traced the soft curves of her breast. Shockwaves of sensation exploded through her.

Trembling, she whispered his name again.

Marc ran his thumb over the demanding centre of her breast. Her breath lodged in her throat as fire scorched along secret pathways from his touch. Although lightning flashed against her closed eyelids and thunder roared around them, nature couldn't produce as powerful a storm as the one that conquered her.

And then Marc lifted his head and with narrowed, blazing eyes watched her realise what she was doing.

Surrendering.

The heat in his gaze changed to coldly crystalline brilliance when shocked horror robbed her face of colour and twisted her mouth into a grimace of self-contempt. Marc had expected his wife to accept the presence of his mistress in their lives. And Paige had kissed him as though he was her one true lover, a man to die for.

'Let me go,' she croaked through numb lips.

Immediately he stepped back and gave her room. 'What do we do about this?' he asked uncompromisingly.

Shame flooded her face in a wash of colour that drained away to leave her skin painfully stretched. Cold and alone and empty, her glittering anticipation crumbling into ashes, she shook her head and said, 'Nothing.' But no sound came out.

However, he understood. She'd expected some protest—something!—*anything* but the hard, humourless smile that curled the corners of his mouth.

'Then we'd better go into the house and forget that it ever happened,' he said courteously. 'The rain's stopped and the storm is over.'

As Paige stepped out of the shelter of the trees the sun burst out in radiance.

From behind her came Marc's voice, sardonic and infuriatingly self-assured. 'But there will be other squalls, and I doubt if either of us will forget.'

'There won't be,' Paige told him stiffly, adding with a swift resentment she instantly regretted, 'As for forget-

GET FREE BOOKS and a FREE MYSTERY GIFT WHEN YOU PLAY THE...

Just scratch off the silver box with a coin. Then check below to see the gifts you get!

SLOT MACHINE GAME!

YES! I have scratched off the silver box. Please send me the four FREE books and mystery gift for which I qualify. I understand I am under no obligation to purchase any books, as explained on the back of this card. I am over 18 years of age.

P3KI

Mrs/Miss/Ms/Mr _____ Initials _____

BLOCK CAPITALS PLEASE

Surname _____

Address _____

_____

_____ Postcode _____

 Worth FOUR FREE BOOKS plus a BONUS Mystery Gift!

Worth FOUR FREE BOOKS!

Worth ONE FREE BOOK!

TRY AGAIN!

Visit us online at www.millsandboon.co.uk

The Reader Service™ — Here's how it works:

NO STAMP NEEDED!

THE READER SERVICE™
FREE BOOK OFFER
FREEPOST CN81
CROYDON
CR9 3WZ

NO STAMP
NECESSARY
IF POSTED IN
THE U.K. OR N.I.

ting—you'll do that easily. Women are expendable, after all.'

A heartbeat of silence pulsed around them before he drawled, 'What exactly do you mean by that?'

'I'm sure you know.'

'And I'm sure I don't.' Iron ran like a threat through his tone. 'Explain it.'

She bit her lip. Her damnable temper had to erupt at the very worst time, summoned by the intense frustration that tore her composure to tatters. If he hadn't lifted his head and looked into her face she'd have willingly co-operated in her own seduction.

This humiliating knowledge spurred her on. 'Simply that whatever you want from women is easily found. It means nothing more than momentary pleasure.'

His smile was cynical, almost cruel. 'Indeed?' he said with cool indifference, and stooped and crushed her startled mouth beneath his.

The kiss was over in a heartbeat, but while it lasted her lips had shaped to his.

'Momentary?' he murmured, his tone insultingly relaxed.

Shame burned like acid, concealing a pain she refused to face. She was too unsophisticated to play teasing, sexual games. Keeping her face averted, she walked beneath the bold heat of the sun and tried to ignore the man beside her.

He said, 'And what makes you think I see sex as a game between men and women? Did Juliette tell you that?'

The ice in his words scraped along her nerves. 'I'd have to be stupid not to know that women are, always obtainable—' her voice invested the word with scorching disdain '—when you're rich.'

'A certain sort of woman,' he agreed silkily. 'But greed

is not exclusive to the female sex—a certain type of man is always on the lookout for rich women. And you're evading my question.'

They had reached the limits of the garden; automatically courteous, he reached to unlatch the gate and stood back to let her go through it first. Moving as carefully as though he were a tiger in ambush, she walked past him.

'You have no right to ask that question,' she said with steady composure. 'My conversations with Juliette were private.'

He said with clinical assurance, 'So she did.'

Paige waited tensely for him to reject the accusation, but he remained silent while they walked through the splendid gardens, past the tennis court and between two large citrus trees, glowing with burnished fruit like a treasure beyond price.

He startled her by observing with a judicial lack of emotion, 'Your father's defection presumably hit you hard, and making friends with Sherry would reinforce your belief that people exploit each other.'

Anger lit her eyes and tightened her lips—lips that still stung from his kisses. 'We've had this conversation before.'

'I'm just surprised that you accept her solution.' He held back a wet branch so that she didn't get drenched. Great drops fell like tears at his touch.

Paige cast him a glinting, dangerous glance. 'She does what she has to,' she said steadily. 'Women do, you know—we survive, and for some of us it's not easy or particularly pleasant.'

'Then why aren't you stripping with your friend on the stage?' He slashed her with a survey as blue and hard as the gleam in a diamond.

Paige stiffened as his gaze travelled from the vulnerable

length of her throat to her breasts, and then on to the apex of her body, assessing the contours of her legs beneath her trousers, and back up to her face, by then pale and set.

He said with brutal frankness, 'You've a good body, and you dance like a dream. You could probably earn as much as she does.'

Paige's teeth ravaged her bottom lip. 'It's not my scene,' she said finally.

'Then how about this—I will pay you to stay with me for—oh, shall we say a year? At the end of the year you'll be free to go.'

Paige gasped, her breath almost strangling her. He couldn't mean it—no, of course he didn't mean it. 'Don't be ridiculous.'

Smoothly, with enough cruel irony in his tone to set her skin crawling, he finished, 'Those kisses made it more than clear that there is nothing ridiculous about the proposition. I'd guess it would take us a year at least to tire of each other.'

Pain blocked her throat. She could only walk beside him and listen to his silkily dispassionate voice tear down dreams she hadn't known she'd been harbouring.

'Of course when it was over I'd make sure you had enough money to set you up in whatever business you desire, and keep you for a couple of years while it was getting onto its feet.' He paused, but when she said nothing he went on, still in that coldly amused tone, 'All you have to do is satisfy me. I can certainly promise to satisfy you.'

'I am not a prostitute,' Paige ground out, staring wretchedly at a hibiscus flower, brazenly scarlet with its silken petals gleaming. She didn't dare look at Marc, because he might guess that just for an instant—for a shameless fraction of a second—she'd been tempted.

'I rest my case.'

She stopped and jerked around to face him, eyes glittering in her stormy face. 'But I don't know what I'd do if I had a baby to look after! Sherry believes that all she's got to offer is her body. She wants to make sure Brodie never has to endure the sort of childhood she had, and to do that she's got to have a financial stake. She's getting it the fastest way she can.'

She stopped, infuriated by the inflexible expression on his boldly marked features. 'And you—' she finished with loathing '—you're a narrow-minded snob.'

His expression didn't change. 'Whereas your loyalty seems to be exceeded only by your gullibility. Women like Sherry move through any level of society. The ones I meet are more sophisticated, but essentially they have the same practical attitude.'

Something in the deep voice caught her attention, yet she couldn't decide what it was. Was he thinking of his mistress?

She began to walk towards the house, saying unsteadily, 'It would probably do you good to be in her shoes for a year. Then you might learn not to judge people.'

Marc watched her march away, shoulders erect, her stiff-legged fury unable to overcome the seductive, entirely unconscious sway of her hips. Fickle sunlight poured over her hair, turning it into a fall of dark honey-amber, still tousled by the rake of his fingers when he'd kissed her. Her skin echoed the colour, softened it and turned it into a pale, delicate glow so that she shimmered like a figurine, rare and precious and too delicate.

Heat slammed through him—heat that resisted the icy chill of logic and common sense. He bit back searing words and followed her, catching her up in two smooth, powerful strides.

At the intersection of two paths presided over by a superb marble Pan, she hesitated, not sure which way to go.

'To the left,' Marc directed abruptly, looking past her down that path. The cold control that had locked his features into stillness altered as he said smoothly, 'Ah, Lauren's arrived. She's an executive in Corbett's. In fact, although you haven't been formally introduced, you've met her—she was with me in Napier. She has a special interest in New Zealand.'

Paige swung around and watched with an oddly kicking heart as the tall woman came towards them. So this *was* the woman who had darkened Juliette's life. She suspected that she knew exactly what that special interest was—the man beside her.

Pain raked her with unsheathed claws; she took in a long, silent breath, stiffened her spine and angled her chin, wounded pride providing the courage to smile as she was introduced to the woman whose mocking voice she'd never forgotten.

Sleekly elegant, Lauren Porter possessed something a lot more special than conventional beauty—intelligence, and a knowledgeable sophistication that irradiated her fine features. And she had the same aura of confidence as Marc, an inbuilt assurance that set Paige's defences slamming up. She looked younger than Marc, but probably only by a couple of years.

Juliette would have had no defences against a woman like this.

After that initial softening Marc's unbreakable control masked his emotions, but his executive gave Paige a warm smile.

'So we meet again. Are you enjoying your visit to the island?' Lauren Porter asked.

'Very much, thank you.' Paige's voice sounded stiff but pleasant.

Before the other woman could answer Marc interpolated smoothly, 'And we're both a little damp, thanks to that last shower. Let's go inside.'

Back in her bedroom, Paige changed and showered and wondered at the smiling regard Marc's mistress had turned on her. She seemed very—well, pleasant. But *pleasant* was a nothing word, emotionless and without juice. And beneath that charming exterior there had to be much more than mere pleasantness.

Raging sexual desire, perhaps.

Paige's hand stole up to touch her lips. She clamped them tight to stop them trembling, feeling as though she'd walked through a barred gate onto a pathway leading down to destruction.

Which was ridiculous; she'd been kissed before.

Not often, she admitted reluctantly. As her mother had sunk into illness her friends had fallen away, so there had been no kisses after the unpractised ones stolen by the occasional boy at high school.

Perhaps her response to Marc was an indication of how utterly green and inexperienced she was; his lovemaking might not be anything special at all.

Perhaps any man might have that effect on her.

She shuddered with disgust, remembering her boss. Well, not *any* man...but any man she wanted. As for Marc; next time—if there was a next time!—his touch set off erotic explosions all through her, she had to remember why she disliked and distrusted him.

If she weakened at all towards him she could expect eventual rejection and bitter desolation.

Changing into jeans and a white shirt, she wondered miserably where Lauren Porter had bought her sleek black trousers and the pure red top made from merino wool as fine as silk. The black jacket over it was certainly leather, and so were the red gloves tucked dashingly into the pocket.

A very classy lady, Paige thought wearily. She examined herself in the mirror, then shrugged. She was no competition.

So why had Marc kissed her senseless? What would Lauren think if she knew? Perhaps a worldly woman wouldn't care how many other lovers he had.

Whereas if he was hers she'd scratch the eyes out of—

'No!' she said as her appalled gaze flew to the hands curling into claws at her sides.

Oh, no. Apart from being the most appalling disloyalty to Juliette, she was so far out of her league she might as well be a sparrow hunted by an eagle.

Not that she liked that idea, either. A nice domestic tabby, she decided with a mocking smile at her idiocy, in the den of a blue-eyed tiger.

Paige swallowed an uncomfortable obstruction in her throat and fastened an interested, alert, uninvolved look to her face before sallying out to confront Marc.

But when she steeled herself to walk casually into the room Marc had told her they'd meet in she found it empty. Not for long, however; the housekeeper arrived hot on her heels.

'I'm sorry,' Mrs Oliver said without preamble, 'but Marc asked me to tell you that there's an emergency—business, not personal—so he won't be able to dine with you tonight.'

Paige fought down the infuriating spasm of disappointment underlying her quick relief. 'I hope it's nothing too bad?'

Mrs Oliver said with complete confidence, 'Marc will

deal with it, whatever it is. He thrives on challenges. Shall I bring dinner here?' She indicated a table at one end of the informal room that shared the same warm, appealing elegance as the rest of the house.

'Thank you. Can I help with anything?'

The older woman smiled at her. 'That's very thoughtful of you, but I'm too set in my ways to work comfortably with anyone else in the kitchen. Dinner will be in half an hour or so. Afterwards, would you like to watch television? Or a film? Marc gets them flown in.'

'That sounds great.'

But later, after she'd made herself eat a delicious meal, sat in a fabulous home theatre and watched a taut, well-acted drama that hadn't yet reached New Zealand, she refused coffee or tea in favour of an early night and walked back to her room feeling stupidly abandoned.

'Ridiculous!' she said sternly, closing the door behind her too vigorously. So Marc admitted to wanting her—that didn't give her licence to develop a humiliating fixation.

His kisses had been dynamite. And her response had been scary. Somehow he'd smashed down all her barriers to reach some hidden, subversive part of her that gloried in the wildness and the heat and the urgent need his touch summoned.

However, although she'd wanted Marc with a desperation that scared the hell out of her, lust wasn't love, so she had no reason to feel this stupid, useless, embarrassing sense of betrayal. Love meant need and dependence and sacrifice—and eventual rejection—whereas lust, a simple physical itch, was much safer.

In fact, if she were an experienced woman she might even be tempted to have an affair with him.

Getting ready for bed, she toyed recklessly with the idea of yielding to the tormenting desperation that ran like hot honey through her body whenever she remembered those moments in his arms. Perhaps indulging in a wild conflagration of passion would eventually exorcise it, because nothing so intense could last—the human frame wasn't equipped to deal with prolonged exposure to such hunger. 'Don't be an idiot,' she scoffed, stamping out of the bathroom. 'Starting your sex life with an arrogant, autocratic, *cheating* magnate would be a very bad move.' Yet an unknown emotion tightened painfully around her heart.

Some time during the evening the housekeeper had removed the white bedspread and replaced the bolster with large, continental pillows. Beside the jug of water on a chest were a bowl of fruit and some crackers.

Clearly Marc gave great thought to his guests' comfort. Not likely, she thought with an ironic smile. Apart from making sure he employed well-trained staff, he probably took it all completely for granted.

Why had he been so determined to fulfil the conditions of Juliette's will?

Her lip curled as she marched across the room. The most cynical answer was the right one; he knew he'd hurt Juliette with his unfaithfulness, so this was a sop to a guilty conscience.

And it wasn't costing him anything—not even time, because he was leaving tomorrow.

Aching with a desolate tiredness, she crawled into bed and switched off the light, waiting impatiently for sleep to shut down the chaos in her mind.

Only to have it play and replay with loving fidelity each delicious, forbidden kiss, every erotic stimulus, from the subtle friction of his shaven jaw to the vivid impact of flame-blue eyes, the experienced, knowledgeable touch of his hand on her breast, the blatant hunger of his hardening body...

Her own body sprang into eager life. Groaning, Paige turned her head into the pillow.

The telephone beside the bed shocked her with a soft, insistent warble. Heart jolting, she bolted upright, groping for the receiver. 'Hello?' she muttered.

Marc said, 'I thought you might like to ring Sherry and reassure her that you got here safely.'

Adrenaline sizzled through Paige like a charge of lightning. 'I—now?' But guilt bit deep; she'd meant to ask if she could contact her flatmate, and she'd been so caught up in her own concerns she'd forgotten.

'It's not late,' he said smoothly. 'I'll put you through.'

Paige opened her mouth to say something—she never knew what—but the number clicked up automatically and within a couple of seconds Sherry said, 'Hello?' into the receiver.

'It's Paige here. How's everything going?'

She relaxed at Sherry's soft, unforced laugh.

'Everything's fine. How are you? What's your guy's place like?'

'He's not my guy,' Paige said automatically.

'He wants to be,' Sherry teased. 'Talk about vibes!'

Paige said curtly, 'We have nothing in common.'

'You mean he's rich and you're not?'

Amongst other things. They also had completely different standards and values. Paige said lightly, 'Yep. Now I know how a fish out of water feels!'

'Rubbish,' her friend said indignantly. 'You'd fit in anywhere—you're pretty and nice and you're clever. What more could anyone want?'

Paige laughed, but Sherry's quick support warmed her. 'Thanks.'

'Still, be careful, all right?' Sherry's voice changed into

an almost maternal warning. 'Men like him aren't used to having women say no to them.'

Paige stated with such utter conviction she startled herself, 'You don't need to worry; he's not the sort to turn ugly. Besides, the long-term girlfriend is here, and they're taking off for parts unknown tomorrow.'

'Oh. Pity,' Sherry said, clearly not convinced.

'The house is lovely—old, but beautifully restored and added to, and only a few steps from a fabulous beach with huge old pohutukawa trees along the beachfront. It will be breathtaking in summer—great crimson domes against the sea. And not another house in sight, although there must be a place for the housekeeper.'

'A housekeeper?' Now Shelley was impressed.

'Yes. And the island is covered in native bush, so from the air it looks like a greenstone heart—fairytale stuff! Marc's helicopter met us at the airport and flew us over.'

'Cool!' Sherry didn't have an envious bone in her body. 'You enjoy it—every minute of it. Don't worry about me and Brodie, we're fine and enjoying our holiday together, so don't think of coming back until you're ready. You might as well make the most of whatever good fortune comes your way.' She paused, then said, 'And, Paige, I've been thinking. If you want to stay—'

'I don't. I'll be back home in a week's time.'

'Oh.' Sherry sounded startled, but she went on swiftly, 'Well, you might see a chance of a job or something there. You haven't had much luck in Napier, so if one comes up, take it. Don't worry about us. As a matter of fact, I think I might be getting a job myself—a *proper* job. I interviewed for it this afternoon—nice people.'

She sounded so elaborately offhand that Paige realised it was a job she wanted very much. 'Where?' she asked. 'Doing what?'

'In the country—well, about twenty kilometres out of Napier. I saw it in the paper after you left, and when I rang they were quite keen.' She gave a little laugh. 'It's light housework and taking care of a couple of kids after school. There's a free flat for me and Brodie.'

'It sounds perfect.' If Sherry got that job, Paige wouldn't be able to afford the unit. She pushed the thought to the furthest reaches of her mind and said heartily, 'I'll keep my fingers crossed for you.'

'Yeah, well, the money's not as good, of course, but I'll be able to save most of it. And it's more wholesome for Brodie to grow up there. Oh-oh, he's stirring. I'd better hang up.' Dropping her voice, Sherry said, 'Have a great time, and for once start looking out for yourself, OK?'

Paige's smile faded as she hung up. She switched off the light again and lay down, blessing the employer who was prepared to look past the stripper to the warm, responsible woman that Sherry was.

The telephone rang again. Lifting herself onto her elbow, Paige stared at it, then slowly reached for the receiver.

Marc asked, 'Is everything all right?'

'Fine, thank you.' She heard Lauren Porter's voice, sharply urgent.

Marc said, 'I'm sorry, I have to go. Goodnight, Paige.'

'Goodnight.'

But it seemed hours that she lay listening to heavy showers hiss across the sea and pounce onto the house. Was the emergency an all-night affair? Or was Marc with Lauren, making love on a bed even bigger than this one?

She turned over onto her stomach, thrusting her face into the pillow, and tried to block out the images that flashed through her brain. Eventually she drifted off to sleep, but she spent the rest of the night tormented by dark, agitated dreams, and woke with a jolt, aching all over, to the sound of the helicopter taking off.

Marc was leaving. Without conscious thought, she bolted out of bed.

CHAPTER EIGHT

BY THE time Paige had pushed the curtains back, and wrestled open the shutters onto the terrace, the sound of the chopper's engines had faded across the sea. The sudden hollowness beneath her ribs was invaded by a pain so acute she had to lean against the wall; narrowing her eyes, she frantically searched for the helicopter.

And when at last she caught the tiny silver glint buzzing across a cloudless sky, she whispered, 'Goodbye,' on a silent sob.

'Good morning,' Marc said from far too close.

Stiff with shock, she whirled around. Clad in well-cut trousers and nothing else, he'd walked out through another set of doors only a few feet from hers. The sun gilded his broad shoulders and magnificent torso and revealed the shadow clinging to his unshaven jaw. He looked like a buccaneer, sexy and sinful and formidably dangerous in every meaning of the word.

Heat exploded deep in the pit of her stomach. Squelching her first impulse to flee back into her bedroom, drag the curtains across and hole up there until the helicopter arrived back to rescue her from such reckless temptation, Paige stood firm and took a deep breath. If only she'd combed her hair before she came out! She could feel it rioting around her head like spun toffee.

Refusing to glance down at the shabby T-shirt she slept in, she said, 'Good morning.' And, while the smile curling his sculpted mouth wreaked untold damage on her nervous system, she blurted, 'Where's the helicopter going?'

110

'It's taking Lauren to Kerikeri. She has to catch the eight o'clock plane to Auckland.'

Dry-mouthed, she said, 'I thought you were leaving with her?'

'I'm not going until after lunch,' he said, almost as though she had the right to ask.

She met his eyes steadily, but couldn't read anything in his enamelled blue eyes and calm, outrageously handsome face.

The smile returned, high voltage this time. 'Did you sleep well?'

Tamping down a wild response, she told him shortly, 'Very well, thank you.' No lie, either. Once she'd chiselled those images from her brain she'd gone under like a drowning victim! But some masochistic urge persuaded her to ask, 'How about you?'

'When I finally got to sleep.' And before she had time to torture herself further with pictures of him in bed with Lauren he said, 'I'm sorry about last night. I had to deal with something that wouldn't wait.'

'It doesn't matter.' A cool breeze from the sea breathed on her, puckering her skin. 'It was a pleasant evening, and I enjoyed the film.'

He frowned. 'You'd better get into some warmer clothes.'

Did he ever miss anything?

He finished, 'I'll see you at breakfast in half an hour.'

'Certainly,' she said crisply, and walked inside, closing the shutters behind her.

Half an hour later he was coming along the passage when she emerged from her bedroom.

'A punctual woman,' he said. He regarded her with sardonic amusement. 'Hungry?'

She had been, but the sight of him, shaven and with his

splendid torso concealed by a shirt that darkened his eyes to smoky sapphires, stole her appetite.

Trying to marshal her tumbling emotions into some sort of order, she went with him to the room where she'd eaten her solitary dinner the night before. The dog Fancy ambled in through the open doors of the terrace to gaze adoringly at Marc, her tail wagging with expectation until he greeted her. Then, politely, she came across and let Paige stroke her head.

'She must miss you when you're away,' Paige observed, approaching the chair Marc held for her.

'I don't think so.' He looked down at the dog with a half-smile. 'I probably miss her more. According to Rose Oliver she sleeps a lot.'

It felt as though a century had gone by since this time yesterday, when she'd been walking the dogs in Napier, Paige thought despairingly as he slid the chair in beneath her.

Well, things *had* happened—she'd flown up here, and she'd kissed Marc Corbett. A truly life-changing event, she mocked.

She surveyed her empty plate with absorbed interest while the scents of breakfast teased her nostrils—toast and bacon, the sweet tang of orange juice straight from the tree, the delicious promise of coffee.

Kisses didn't have to mean anything, common sense assured her bracingly.

But Marc's kisses had spun her world off its axis. When she'd caught fire her surrender had shattered her life's safe, prosaic foundations into splinters.

'Something wrong?' Marc enquired. 'No, I remember— it normally takes you a while to wake up in the morning. Do you need a kick-start—coffee, perhaps?'

Sitting mute as a fish was hardly cool. She said evenly, 'Coffee helps.'

'Pour yourself a cup, then. And one for me, if you don't mind—black.'

It figured. Glad to have something to do, she lifted the pot and, while he made a sortie to the sideboard, carefully poured two large cups of coffee.

When he sat down she glanced at his plate, and in a voice she hoped sounded amused and light, asked, 'Do you eat porridge every morning?'

'At home I do.'

'Like father, like son.' The moment she said the words she'd have given anything to call them back. His father's nickname of the Robber Baron hadn't been affectionately given.

Marc shrugged. 'In matters of breakfast,' he confirmed blandly. 'What would you like?'

'Fruit, thank you, and toast.'

She got up and helped herself. Spooning yoghurt over tamarillos, she wondered angrily how just being in the same room as him made her respond so much more vividly; the yoghurt blazed like white fire against the ruby-coloured fruit, and the air stroking her skin was potent with fragrance.

While she ate Marc made polite conversation, his ease chipping away at her self-confidence. If those searing kisses had meant anything to him he'd be like her, almost raw with awareness, instead of giving off an aura of self-possession that meant he was fully in control.

'As the weather has settled we'll go around the island this morning,' he said urbanely. 'It will give you some idea of what the place looks like from the sea.'

It took all her will power to answer sedately, 'That's very kind, but you don't have to entertain me.'

His brows rose. 'It would be a pity if you don't see some of the Bay while you're up here.'

'You don't have to feel obliged—'

'Paige,' he said, his pleasant tone failing to hide a steely note, 'I won't kiss you again.'

A tumult of colour scorched her skin. Outside a dove cooed seductively, the soft sounds floating across the terrace and in through the wide doors.

'You won't get the chance,' she said, hurrying the words out so fast they arrived joined together. She breathed in deeply, and asked with stilted steadiness, 'Is there any chance of me seeing Juliette's legacy this morning?'

She felt greedy, and somehow sordid, but she wasn't going to pretend that this was a simple, carefree holiday, with yesterday's exchange of kisses a diversion to be easily ignored.

'Certainly,' he said with a hint of frost in his tone. It had disappeared when he said, 'I'll make a bargain with you.'

Startled, she looked up into eyes as cool and crystalline as the heart of a sapphire. 'What?' she asked, oddly breathless.

'I'll get Rose to bring the box along to your room after we come back. In return, promise to stop looking at me as though I'm going to leap on you. I'm sorry for kissing you yesterday.' His eyes were opaque blue gems against the tanned skin of his angular face as he scanned her face. When she moved uncomfortably in her seat, he said calmly, 'I won't make any excuses—you are deliciously desirable, and I temporarily lost my head—but it won't happen again.'

Because he'd spent last night in Lauren Porter's arms? Perhaps he did feel some loyalty towards his long-term mistress after all.

And she was very happy about his promise, Paige told herself, lying like an expert. 'All right,' she said gruffly.

'Now, do you think you'll be able to eat your breakfast instead of pushing it around the plate?'

Well, of course he was amused. He probably thought she was gauche and green and still wet behind the ears. No doubt he was kicking himself for losing his head temporarily yesterday, and this hideously embarrassing and painful conversation was his attempt at damage limitation.

'Yes,' she said stiffly, and began to force the food past the obstruction in her throat.

Marc's motor cruiser was smaller than the big yacht; nevertheless, Paige decided, eyeing the galley and comfortable cabin, it was nothing like the family boats owned by so many New Zealanders. As well as looking like a rich man's toy it exuded modern technology and luxury.

An uncharacteristic melancholy stole some of the warmth and colour from the day.

'Do you know anything about boats?' Marc asked, standing back to let her climb a set of steps from the deck to a high cabin above the main one.

'I can row,' she told him, going up nimbly. 'That's about it.'

At the top of the stairs he said, 'This is the flybridge.' He indicated an impressive bank of dials and screens in front of a leather chair fixed to the deck. 'Sit down and we'll get moving.'

Leather sofas stretched around the sides beneath windows that provided a panoramic view on three sides. The fourth opened towards the rear of the boat. Gingerly Paige sat down and watched Marc, big and dark and competent, take the wheel and deal with the array of dials.

Once they were out of the Bay and moving slowly down

the coast he said, above the noise of the engine, 'Glad I made you put on a jacket?'

She smiled and bent to stroke Fancy's gleaming head. 'Yes.'

'It's always colder on the sea. Would you like to try a stint behind the wheel?'

She hesitated, met a gleaming challenge in his eyes, and shrugged. 'Provided you don't abandon me there,' she said carefully.

'Trust me.'

Into a silence heavy with unspoken thoughts, she said, 'I hope you know the way.'

'I know the Bay like the back of my hand.'

He stepped aside and showed her how to hold the wheel. Trying not to notice that he avoided touching her, for a glorious half-hour she steered the boat with Marc beside her as he showed her his island.

Finally he took over again and brought them into a small cove where white sand gleamed against a thick forest of cabbage trees. Behind their spiky, surreal tufts of leaves reared forest giants, tall and dark and sombre as they climbed the hills backing the beach. Massive, sprawling pohutukawas clung to the cliffs of both headlands, their reddish aerial roots dangling in the spray.

The sound of the engine muted into a low throb, barely noticeable. 'Cabbage Tree Bay,' Marc told her.

'I can see why.' She admired the clumps of tall-stemmed plants, each slender trunk finished by a tuft of long, strap-like leaves. 'It's a lily—did you know? The biggest lily in the world.'

When he smiled her heart performed an aerial ballet in her chest.

'I didn't know. My father told me that the Maori and

the early settlers used to eat the tender end of the inner leaves, which is why it's called a cabbage tree.'

'They were a prosaic lot, our forebears,' she agreed, ruthlessly ignoring the expanding bubble of excitement in her breast.

'Have you always been interested in plants?'

Paige fiddled with a button on the jacket she'd discarded. 'Always. I used to drive my mother crazy long before I went to school. I'd haul up her seeds and seedlings to see what was happening under the ground. When I got older I was fascinated by the whole miracle of it—how you could plant a tiny seed and this glorious plant would grow from it.'

'So you're more interested in plants than in landscaping?' Marc asked with a lift of his brows.

She concealed her self-consciousness with a half-smile. 'There are two sorts of gardeners: artists who paint pictures with plants, and jewellers who treat each plant like a precious gem and try to find the perfect setting for it. I'm the second sort.'

When the silence stretched too long she risked a glance upwards. He was looking above her head towards the shore, his expression hard and ruthlessly aggressive.

Chilled, Paige felt Fancy push her head into the palm of her hand. Without looking down, she stroked the dog's head.

Marc said, 'Would you go to university if you could afford it?'

She shrugged. 'Of course. But it's not going to happen in the near future.'

He leaned forward and pressed a button. Startled, she heard a chain rattle.

'It's the anchor going down,' he told her. 'What sort of career do you have in mind?'

Career? She was silent, realising that her fight to survive had banished every dream she'd once had into a grey limbo.

Eventually she said slowly, 'I'd like to hybridise plants. New Zealand does so well in that field because we can grow such a wide variety. There's nothing I'd get more pleasure from than seeing a plant of my breeding flower for the first time.'

The silence that followed her words assumed overtones she couldn't decipher.

With a narrow smile Marc nodded at the dinghy on the stern. 'I'll put the dinghy out and you can show me how well you row.'

'Why?' Paige knew she sounded bewildered.

Blue eyes gleaming, he said smoothly, 'Because you might feel like puddling around in it. The homestead is just over the hill there; it's an easy row from there to here. Satisfy me that you know what you're doing and you can take the dinghy out whenever you want to, provided you wear a life jacket.'

Paige picked up the life jacket he'd given her and put it on, then ran lightly down the steps from the flybridge. After Marc had showed her how to heave the rubber dinghy over the stern he ignored Fancy's excited barks and stood watching as with calm competence Paige worked the oars to move the little craft away from the cruiser.

It had been over a year since she'd rowed anywhere, but it was like riding a bike; you didn't forget. This dinghy was wider and more clumsy than Lloyd's old plyboard one, but it slipped through the water far more easily.

Under Marc's assessing gaze she rowed around the cruiser and then out into the centre of the Bay, returning when the palms of her hands indicated that this was as much work as they were prepared to deal with that day.

'You can row,' he said as she shipped the oars and brought the dinghy against the stern of the boat. 'Stop whining, Fancy—see, she's back.'

Paige took his outstretched hand and was hauled up, up, up—almost into his arms. He let her go just before she got there and smiled down at her, his eyes narrowed into gleaming sapphire slivers.

'Fancy loves going out in boats,' he said, a note of mockery threading through his tone, as though he could read the mute, dark frustration that weighted Paige's limbs. He glanced at his watch. 'We'd better get back.'

Neither spoke in the few minutes it took the cruiser to reach Home Bay. Marc was withdrawing, his expression stern, as though the world beyond this idyllic island was already taking him over with its demands and pressures.

But as they walked up to the house he said, 'Promise me you'll ask Rose Oliver whenever you want to take the dinghy out. She was born on the island and she knows it well. She's also pretty good on the weather.'

'I'll tell her where I'm going and listen to her if she says it's not safe,' Paige said evenly. 'I'm not stupid.'

He gave her a glinting look, hard mouth curling into a smile that sent a million tiny darts of pleasurable excitement through her. 'Far from it.' And as they reached the door he said, 'I'll send Rose along to your room with Juliette's parcel.'

In her bedroom, Paige sat down on the chair, struggling against a stupid urge to cry. She stared tensely across the subtle, sophisticated room; through the dark wooden slats of the shutters the sea danced and glittered in shards of pure, brilliant colour.

Someone knocked on the door.

Mrs Oliver carried a small box—one Paige thought she

recognised. Why, she thought in bewilderment, would Juliette leave me her mother's bracelet?

'Mr Corbett asked me to bring you this,' the older woman said. 'And there's this too.' She looked down at an envelope.

'Thank you,' Paige said thinly. She held out her hand, and after a moment's hesitation the housekeeper gave both the box and the envelope to her.

Clutching them, Paige backed into the room and closed the door, waiting long, hushed seconds before putting the box down on the white cover of the huge bed. A dark fingertip of premonition touched her soul.

'Open it!' she told herself, but it took her several more minutes before she overcame the sick panic clogging her chest and unsealed the lid.

She blinked back tears. A gold chain-link bracelet met her eyes, its heart-shaped lock set in small diamonds.

As a child she'd admired the little bracelet extravagantly, convinced it was the most beautiful thing she'd ever seen. Juliette had occasionally let her wear it, and she'd strutted around feeling like a princess.

And now Juliette was dead, and this was all she had of her—the bracelet, and the letter that had come with it. With tear-blurred eyes she picked up the envelope and read her name, written in Juliette's distinctive handwriting. Paige tore it open and took out the note inside. Slowly, carefully, she unfolded the paper.

Dearest P, if you ever read this it will mean that Marc was right to persuade me to make a will! Sorry it has taken a couple of years to get this to you—there is a reason for it, but it is not important. If it ever does become important, you'll find out why.

I know Marc will make it possible for you to stay here

at Arohanui, no matter what your circumstances are now. Have fun—and that is an order. I want you to stay for a week because you work far too hard, and I know that you will not have had a proper holiday since your father left.

Are you wondering if I have any words of wisdom for you? Sorry, I have not. Just that you should grab life and enjoy it—especially the time you're spending here. Lots of love, J.

She'd added a PS.

You were always my best friend, as well as the little sister I never had.

Clutching the letter, Paige got to her feet and walked across to the window. She stared out with unseeing eyes until another knock at the door broke into the shell of silence.

Silently she dashed across the room and stuffed the letter beneath the coverlet.

Sure enough, Marc stood outside the door. 'You've been crying,' he accused, his voice clipped and hard.

'No. Just—remembering.' Before she could stop herself, she asked, 'Was Juliette happy?'

He looked at her with an enigmatic hooded gaze. 'She was always bright and serene, and she seemed perfectly happy.'

In spite of Lauren's presence in his life? Not likely.

Paige said 'Why did she insist I come up here to collect the bracelet?'

'I have no idea.' He paused, then added, 'You didn't see much of her after she went away to boarding school, did you?'

'No,' Paige said distantly.

'Nevertheless, you must have had a strong friendship, to last so long and bridge distance and the years so successfully. Juliette always knew what she wanted, and she wanted you here.' Marc glanced at his watch. 'Lunch is ready—come and have it with me.'

He didn't ask her what had been in the letter—not then, and not before he left. Paige sat on her bed listening to the helicopter engines fade into the distance, bitter tears aching at the back of her eyes and clogging her throat.

That night Marc rang from Australia, and the next night from Singapore, and the evening after that from Tokyo in Japan. The calls continued, and Paige found herself waiting expectantly through each lovely, lonely day for his ring.

He didn't spend much time talking, but with the brutal intensity of physical awareness muted by distance she discovered a new Marc; he told her a little of his day, described each city with economy and a flair for bringing it to life. He joked with her, teased her a little, and asked her what she'd done.

She stored small discoveries to tell him—that the fruit on the loquat tree was being eaten by a pair of large, beautiful native pigeons who sat on the branches and peered interestedly down at her with heads tipped to one side. She told him she'd been rowing around Home Bay with Fancy for a figurehead, that Mrs Oliver was making guava jelly and had shown her how bake the perfect pavlova.

Later she'd realise that she fell in love with him during those telephone calls, but for now she just knew that they satisfied something deep inside her.

On her second to last night at Arohanui he didn't ring. Painfully disappointed, she resisted the stupid feeling that because she couldn't talk it over with Marc her day had been wasted and barren.

The next morning she came in from the terrace after breakfast and said to the housekeeper, 'Summer's come early this year.'

'It's certainly a glorious day.' Mrs Oliver smiled, efficiently continuing her dusting.

'I thought I might row around to Cabbage Tree Bay,' Paige said, tracing the outline of a flower on a blue Japanese bowl.

Her sleep had been punctuated by long periods of wakefulness when her brain had twisted and turned in futile, anguished resentment. In the end she'd had to accept that she'd allowed herself to become subtly dependent on Marc for—oh, not her happiness, but for an intangible support.

She needed exercise, something physically draining, to stop her remembering that after she left Arohanui she'd never see him again.

Mrs Oliver nodded. 'The forecast is excellent. I'll pack you a lunch.'

'Thanks, but you've got your own work to do. I'll make it.'

'It's no problem,' the housekeeper said, casting a knowledgeable eye across the sky. 'Start back about two o'clock; at half-tide a current sets in around the headlands on that side of the island, and you won't want to be caught in it. Once you get out to sea there's nothing between here and South America.'

Half an hour later Paige stacked a change of clothes, sunscreen, her hat and enough food and drink for a regimental exercise into the dinghy. Fancy got in, taking up her usual position in the bow.

'Here's her leash,' the housekeeper said, handing it over. She smiled at Paige's surprise. 'There are kiwis on the island, and they're fatally attractive to dogs. Last summer Marc had a run-in with some yachties who brought their Jack Russells ashore in Cabbage Tree Bay; he sent them packing in no time. Fancy's obedient, but even she finds it hard to resist kiwis, and you might want to take her for a walk.'

'OK.' Paige put it in with the pile. 'I look as though I'm doing a Robinson Crusoe,' she observed, smiling. 'I hope you don't expect me to eat all that?'

'You'll be surprised. Sea air makes you hungry.' As Paige got into the dinghy Mrs Oliver said, 'You're not going to swim by yourself?'

'No, I haven't got my togs with me.' She organised Fancy and the oars. 'Don't worry, I know how to deal with the water. I lived beside a river for years.'

Mrs Oliver nodded. 'If anything goes wrong, just stay at Cabbage Tree and I'll send my husband for you.'

'OK.' Paige waved and set off.

CHAPTER NINE

AT THE Bay Paige and a leashed Fancy explored the grove of cabbage trees, and when the sun reached its full height Paige sat down on a rug beneath a sprawling pohutukawa and confronted lunch.

It looked and smelt delicious; Rose Oliver was a superb cook. Yet Paige's appetite refused to be aroused. In the end she ate a slice of perfect bacon and egg pie, followed it with the scented, custardy white flesh of a small cherimoya fruit, drank lime juice and water, and looked helplessly at the rest of the food.

Fancy lay a few feet away, eyes fixed on the hamper. She'd already drunk her fill from the small stream that trickled into the sea between the cabbage trees.

'We'd better not waste it all, I suppose. And you've done a lot of dashing about and swimming,' Paige said, and fed her a sandwich.

Tomorrow she was leaving this beautiful place, this dog she'd come to love, and the man who owned both island and dog. She wouldn't come back, and he wouldn't seek her out.

Even if he did, she'd refuse him. With Lauren Porter still in his life, Paige knew that the most he could offer her was less than she wanted.

After a glance at her watch she lay down on the rug and watched the sun dazzle across the sea. She had time to rest before she needed to set off again for Home Bay. Firmly, she closed her eyes.

Not a good idea. Helplessly, without mercy, her mind

125

replayed everything Marc had ever said to her, every touch, each eloquent lift of his brow, the stunning brilliance of his eyes, his heart-shaking smile, the angular, powerful symmetry of his face...

And the way she'd gone up in flames when they'd kissed. The violent, incandescent heat of sensation he'd summoned so effortlessly.

She startled Fancy by getting abruptly to her feet. 'Come on, let's go,' she said raggedly.

The dog snatched up a stick from the sand and dropped it at Paige's feet. Paige sighed, but said, 'Well, why not? I suppose you're missing Marc too.'

Ears pricked, Fancy looked around, as though expecting him.

'He won't come back until I've gone,' Paige told her drearily, and picked up the stick.

Although the very simple game involved only hurling the stick into the waves and watching Fancy retrieve it, kill it on the sand and then bring it back to her, it should burn off some of the reckless energy that pulsed through her.

And perhaps it might keep at bay for a few minutes the secret unhappiness that had stolen like a thief into her heart.

She strode along the beach towards the rocky headland that separated this beach from Home Bay, trying to smile as Fancy pounced on the stick before dancing it back through the tiny waves, golden hair flying, sheer joy in every movement.

Pain gripped her. After tomorrow she'd never see the dog again. She'd never see Mrs Oliver, or her silent, shy husband, never see the vivid garden and the lovely, gracious house at its heart.

Never see Marc, her heart whispered.

Once more Paige threw the stick, then set off towards the dinghy, trying to banish the bitter taste of loss.

She stopped, shading her eyes to watch the dog. Sunlight sultry with the promise of summer beat down on her head and shoulders. The hollow emptiness eating into her self-sufficiency terrified her.

She had no idea when she'd made the decision never to rely on another person for her happiness; it hadn't been a conscious one. Living with a mother whose sense of self-hood had depended completely on the man she'd married had produced that unspoken determination to keep her own identity intact.

And now it was under threat. Marc's potent masculinity had bulldozed through her defences, but that was only part of the problem; she wanted much more from him than the promise of magnificent sex. She wanted the companionship he'd given her in those telephone calls—she wanted a future with him.

A shiver tightened her skin, chilled her heart. She crossed her arms and rubbed from her wrists to her elbows, staring blindly out to sea.

'I'm not in love with Marc Corbett,' she said aloud, despising the sound of her thin, unsure voice.

This acute physical awareness wasn't love, and neither was her fascination with him. Naturally she found him interesting to talk to—intelligence always intrigued her. So did competence. And Marc was nothing if not competent.

If he'd been born without that solid wealth behind him he'd have made it for himself. Articles in the financial pages praised his raw ability and dynamic initiative, tempered by a disciplined, incisive brain and will; they were his defining qualities, not the results of his privileged background.

'And don't forget the fact that he looks like some romantic dream,' she said on a whiplash of self-contempt.

Shaking her head, she narrowed her eyes against the brilliant light. The more she let Marc invade her mind, the greater power she yielded to him.

Frowning, she focused on the water, trying to pick out the stick in the shimmering, deceptive webs of gold the sun spun on the surface of the sea. Fancy was swimming steadily on.

'Ah, there it is,' Paige muttered, then drew in a quick breath.

The stick had acquired momentum, and was moving slowly, purposefully away from the beach. Squinting against the sun, Paige realised that it had been caught in a current.

She cupped her mouth and shouted, 'Fancy, come back! Get back here!'

But Fancy ignored her. And she too was being dragged inexorably towards the rocky end of the far headland.

Fear coagulated in an icy pool beneath Paige's ribs. Once past the cliffs there was nothing between Fancy and the open sea.

Marc loved this dog; if she'd thrown sticks along the beach, instead of into the water, Fancy would be safely on firm ground.

Paige raced over the hot sand to the dinghy. It took her precious moments to pull on and secure the life jacket, but she didn't dare go out without it. And it seemed to take an age to drag the dinghy to the water's edge.

Once it was floating she heaved it seawards with all her strength and flung herself in, snatching up the oars to row as hard and as steadily as she could. Within a couple of minutes she heard the current chuckle under the boat, and felt its inexorable grip carry her towards the dog. A brisk wind whipped her hair into her eyes; she shook it free and concentrated on getting to Fancy.

From what she remembered of the tour Marc had given her, the headland straightened out into a long line of cliffs facing the open sea, rock stacks cluttering their base. Although the sea couldn't be more calm, there'd be no safe harbour there, so she'd have to make it back to Cabbage Tree Bay. And with wind and tide against her that could take some effort.

Fortunately that combination of wind and current meant she got to Fancy before the dog exhausted herself.

'All right, girl,' she said, steadying the little craft against the current; she shipped the oars and leaned over to grab Fancy's collar.

'Up, girl,' she coaxed, and hauled.

It took a couple of heaves, but Fancy's scrabbling co-operation and the dinghy's inherent stability finally brought the dog safely in—where, of course, she promptly shook herself, drenching the only other inhabitant.

'Sit *down*, you daft dog! We have to get back.' Paige risked a glance at the headland, now ominously close, and wished fervently that the dinghy had come equipped with an anchor.

'Well, it hasn't,' she said, beginning the row back to Cabbage Tree Bay. To hearten herself she told Fancy, now in her usual place as figurehead, 'It's do-able. We'll just take it steadily.'

But the current showed its teeth. And the dinghy, so stable and safe, caught enough wind to make progress slow and difficult. After ten minutes Paige glanced up and realised with an abrupt arrow of foreboding just how far she still had to go.

She was only just making headway against that lethal

combination of tide and wind; if either increased in strength she'd be swept out to sea.

Setting her jaw, she concentrated on rowing evenly, letting her mind concentrate on getting the dinghy a little closer to land with each stroke.

Where the hell were the boats that usually dotted the Bay? She could see sails, and some motor cruisers, but they were all too far away to be hailed and none came closer.

'It's a conspiracy,' she muttered, trying to smile at the absurd idea.

The muscles in her shoulders were beginning to burn resentfully when Fancy barked. Paige cast a glance over her shoulder, and if she'd had any energy to spare might have cheered at the sight of the motor cruiser purling around the headland that separated Cabbage Tree Bay from Home Bay.

Waving frantically, she croaked above the growing roar of its engine, 'There, old girl, everything's fine now! We're safe!'

An alteration in the pitch of the engines confirmed that the driver had seen her and answered her call for help. But, just in case, she kept rowing. The big cruiser idled closer; frowning, she scanned its lines, then looked up into the flybridge. Her pulses raced when she recognised Marc behind the wheel.

Such potent, overwhelming delight blazed through her that she realised just how much she'd been fooling herself.

'Oh, God,' she whispered, face white beneath her hat. 'What have you *done*?'

Limp with reaction, she shipped the oars and waited until the cruiser eased to a halt between them and the flow of the current. At the helm, Marc cut the engines to a mere throb in the water.

Paige waited tensely as he manoeuvred the big craft with skilful, delicate precision; a couple of times she had to use the oars, until eventually the dinghy was swept gently against the diving platform at the stern. He left the engines idling and came rapidly down from the flybridge, hauling the dinghy onto its platform with raw energy that spoke of strong emotion.

'Are you all right?' he demanded, his voice abrasive with anger.

Paige looked up into his blazing eyes. 'Fine,' she said tonelessly.

'Get out and I'll deal with Fancy.'

He made it sound easy, but when she tried to stand up her legs buckled like straws. Strong hands grabbed her and hauled her up into the cockpit. Violently tempted to collapse against him, she forced herself upright.

'I'm all right,' she muttered. 'Why have my legs given way? It's my arms and shoulders that have done all the work.'

'Shock.' He plonked her down onto a padded bench and turned to fasten the dinghy after ordering, 'Don't move.'

By now Fancy was aboard, frisking around Marc until he spoke with crisp authority to her. When he bent to deal with a rope Paige watched the muscles in his shoulders bunch and flex, appalled at the power of the sexual instinct in humans. Although waves of tiredness were draining the energy from her, something feral and uncontrolled stirred in the depths of her body. She'd have to be dead, she thought, her palms clammy with fear, not to respond to him.

Marc straightened and gave her a very level, very blue glare. 'Why didn't you anchor and wait for someone to come looking for you?'

'There's no anchor in the dinghy.'

His jaw hardened and he swore beneath his breath. 'I'm sorry. From now on there will be,' he said grimly.

Fancy chose that moment to shake herself again, sending drops of water flying around her like silver bullets.

Paige watched spots darken Marc's fine cotton shirt and the tailored trousers that clung to his lean hips and long legs, and started to laugh helplessly. For that moment the world shone with the promise of delight, because Marc had come home.

His hard face relaxed into a grin, and her laughter faded as she realised with a spasm of sheer, mindless panic that she'd fallen in love with him.

Common sense warned her that she didn't know him well enough. A deeper, more primitive instinct told her she'd loved him—painfully, hopelessly, fiercely—since the moment she'd first seen him.

Some hidden part had recognised him as the man she could give her heart to. And she had; in spite of trying so hard to convince herself that it was nothing more than a crude sexual urge, she'd always known that she loved Marc.

She turned her head sideways to hide the tears that stung her eyes.

But he'd seen. 'You're exhausted,' he said, his amusement obliterated. 'Come into the cabin—I'll make you a drink.'

'I'm wet,' she blurted.

'So am I.' When he still didn't move he picked her up, ignoring her squeak of astonishment to shoulder his way into the main cabin.

Paige blinked desperately, fighting the lure of that strong shoulder. 'It was my fault,' she muttered. 'I was throwing a stick for Fancy and it got caught in the current off Cabbage Tree Bay and she took off.'

'So you rescued her. It's all right.' He sat her down on one of the seats and stood back, his eyes searching her face. 'Do you want a shower?'

Paige could have killed for a shower, but she had no other clothes to get into, and the thought of climbing back into salty wet clothes was distasteful. 'I'll wait until we get back ho—to the house.'

Scarlet with humiliation, she closed her eyes. She had almost called the homestead home—as though she had some claim to the place!

She felt him look at her, but kept her eyes obstinately closed. However, when she heard soft sounds from the galley she forced herself onto her feet, wondering why her body felt like lead.

'Sit down,' he said, arriving with a glass of very pale orange juice.

She looked at him with a spark of defiance. 'If I stay there I might never get up again.'

'You will,' he said coolly. 'You don't give up.'

She accepted the glass. 'I try not to.'

'We have that in common,' he said, and put a hand on her shoulder, urging her back onto the banquette. 'Stay there until you've got some liquid into you. It's water with a splash of orange juice to flavour it. Straight juice isn't good for anyone who's dehydrated.'

'It looks wonderful,' she said, abruptly dry-mouthed and incredibly thirsty. 'But I don't need flavouring for water; I like the taste.' She sipped slowly.

His gaze burned like a blue flame. 'Honest and straightforward,' he said curtly. 'Yet you're complex too, layer after layer after layer, and you resist every attempt to peel you back.'

Deluged by a slow, simmering tide of honeyed sensation, she veiled her eyes with her lashes. 'You make me sound like an onion. Peeling them makes people cry.'

'Some men might take that as a challenge.' His mouth curved in a smile that had mockery and speculation blended in equal parts.

'I'm not up to challenges at the moment,' she returned promptly.

'How do you feel? How stiff are your arms and shoulders?'

She wriggled experimentally. 'Not too bad,' she said, surprised.

'You're probably fitter than you think. Show me your hands.'

Blinking, she held them out. He startled her by taking them in his and turning them over so that he could inspect the palms. A sharp sizzle of electricity banished exhaustion; she drew in a sharp breath and had only just enough will power to force them to lie limply in his.

He felt it too, that hidden, dangerous warmth. Sparks glinted in his eyes and he let her go, saying harshly, 'Another five minutes or so and you'd have had raw patches. When we get home I'll get you some cream for those blisters. Stay there and drink your water slowly while I get us back.'

Silently she watched him go out and up the set of stairs that led to the flybridge. Her breath eased out between her lips and her heart-rate steadied, although it still raced. And, because it was inexpressibly pleasant to be looked after by Marc, she did as she was told, sipping slowly in bemused compliance.

Too soon, however, she began to swelter. She got up and stripped off the life jacket, then went out into the breeze. Fancy was snoozing in the cockpit; she opened one eye as Paige went up the steps to the flybridge.

'Oh,' she said, startled because they were in Cabbage
Tree Bay. 'I thought we were going back to the homestead.'

The anchor went into the water with another swift outcry
of chain. Marc gave her a keen glance that settled into a
scrutiny. 'It won't take us a moment to pick up your gear.
I'll do it; you and Fancy can stay on board. You look
feverish.'

She raised a self-conscious hand to her flushed face.
'Just a bit hot; I was stewing in the life jacket.' She cleared
her throat and found an innocuous subject. 'Fancy looks
very relaxed. I hope she's all right—she was in the water
for quite a long time.'

'She spends summers mostly in the water. She'll be fine.
You'll be the one who'll be stiff tomorrow morning,' Marc
said, a definite note of reserve in the words.

'I don't think so. One thing taking care of a baby does
is strengthen your arms and shoulders.'

She squinted into the sun and he said, 'Go down and
get into the cabin. You're turning slightly pink, and the
reflection from the water will make it worse.'

He watched her walk to the top of the companionway
and disappear, using her hands carefully. No sign of stiff-
ness yet; she moved freely, with the swaying natural grace
he'd noticed the first time he'd seen her—an unconscious,
elemental invitation to every male in sight. His groin
stirred and he turned back to the wheel with a silent, im-
patient oath.

This, he thought with biting irritation, was getting to be
inconvenient.

It had been a bitch of a trip. He'd been presented with
a clear case of corruption by one of his senior executives,
and apart from his cold fury at the deception tidying it up
was going to cost; keeping it quiet was going to be damned

near impossible. As well, a subsidiary in Asia had managed to offend someone very important in the government, which had meant a side trip to smooth things over there.

Yet for the first time he'd had to fight to keep his mind on the issues. It had exasperated him; he'd resented this woman's ability to infiltrate an area of his life that had always been inviolate.

So he'd come back early, and realised just how much Paige had subverted his mind when Rose Oliver told him she wasn't there. He'd taken the launch out because it was the quickest way to get to her.

And his blood had run like ice in his veins when he'd rounded the point and seen her rowing valiantly across the current.

The sooner they went to bed the better, he decided bleakly. Then he'd be able to get her out of his system.

He set off down the companionway, but Paige met him at the door of the cabin.

'You took a bottle of beer out of the fridge,' she said. 'Do you want it?'

He'd intended to drink it, until touching her hands had driven the idea completely from his mind. 'Thanks.' He lifted the small cold bottle to his mouth to take a good gulp, relishing the honest taste and the refreshing chill of the liquid.

'I didn't know you were coming home today,' she said out of the blue. She was keeping her head turned away on the pretext of looking at her juice, but her knuckles were white against the frosted glass.

'Just as well I did,' he said curtly. 'I won't tell you what I felt when I saw you being carried out to sea by the current.'

Her full mouth quivered, then tightened. 'I was making

headway,' she objected. 'I'd have got there. But I was very glad to see the boat come around the point.'

'The most sensible thing would have been to let Fancy go. A dog's life is not as valuable as a human's.'

Paige's head shot up. 'Intellectually I know that, but I couldn't just let her drown.'

'You're too soft for your own good,' he said drily, eyes very blue as he surveyed her.

'Ha!' The word and the smile that accompanied it were pure challenge.

'A woman who gave up her chance of a career to stay at home and care for her mother, then asked a pregnant down-on-her-luck stripper to move in has to be soft-hearted,' he pointed out ironically.

'How did you know that?'

'Sherry told me you rescued her from almost certain destitution.'

'Rubbish!' she interposed robustly.

'When her husband left her. You offered her a bed, helped her get benefit from the government, and you sat with her during her labour and the birth with all the devotion of a sister.'

'Who wouldn't?' she asked matter-of-factly.

'Not everyone would have taken in a stripper,' he said drily.

Made uncomfortable by his keen scrutiny, Paige shrugged. 'She stopped stripping as soon as she got pregnant. And all she needed was support.'

His brow lifted. 'For which she's eternally grateful, as she should be. She also made sure I knew that while you were soft she was not, and more or less warned me to watch myself.'

Paige's jaws met with an audible click, damming the hot words that threatened to spill out.

'Your eyes turn pure green when you're angry,' he said conversationally. 'And they gleam gold when you're aroused. It's like being drowned in fire. I'll see you in ten minutes or so.'

Stunned, she watched him free the dinghy and push it into the water, tell Fancy severely that she wasn't going with him, and row for the shore.

He was back in the ten minutes he'd promised, and unloaded her gear onto the cruiser with another stern word to Fancy, who showed signs of wanting to leap into the water again. He looked up as Paige came out of the cabin to help.

'Stay out of the sun until we get back to Home Bay,' he said austerely.

'Yes, sir.'

One dark brow lifted. 'You're not up to it,' he said softly, and went up to the flybridge.

Once the wooden planks of the Home Bay jetty were safely under feet, Paige smiled in Marc's general direction and said, 'I'll have that shower now.'

'I'll see you later.'

Which sounded ominous. Keeping her face and eyes averted, she picked up the rug and her bag and walked steadfastly away from him.

CHAPTER TEN

MARC caught her up as she reached the door of the house. 'Get under the shower and let the water play on your shoulders and back. You know how to alter the head setting?' At her nod he said, 'Stay under it for as long as you can. I'll send Rose along with that cream for your hands.'

Safe at last in her bathroom, Paige leant into the heavy pulse of the spray, trying to relax as the jets massaged away the ache in her upper arms and shoulders. Although the pummelling hot water brought her superficial ease, a deep inner tension still knotted her nerves.

What a naïve, weak-willed idiot she was! Somehow, in spite of everything she'd done to prevent it, she'd allowed herself to fall in love with Marc Corbett, world-famous tycoon and heartbreaker. Helpless against her hidden desires, she'd let herself be carried along by a force of nature, and inevitably she'd succumbed.

'Like so many other women,' she muttered, pushing her wet hair back from her face. 'Like Lauren.'

A profound grief shadowed her soul. She couldn't give way to it because she still had the rest of the evening and the night to get through, not to mention tomorrow morning before she left for Napier. Marc had organised it all; at nine the helicopter would take her across to Kerikeri, and the same executive jet that had brought her to Arohanui would take her away.

Only this time he wasn't coming with her.

Choking back a sob, she grimly washed the sweat and the salt from her hair. 'I can cope,' she said beneath her breath. But the words echoed with bitterness, and she added silently, *Because I have to. I'm not going to let myself end up like my mother, so fixated on one man that life without him was a dead end.*

Eventually, when her hands started to wrinkle, she got out and wrapped herself in a large white bath towel before picking up the hairdryer. The play of warm air on her head normally soothed her, but not now. Raw grief waited like a predator, ready to catch her the moment she let her guard down.

She'd just finished when she heard the knock on the door. Tightening the knot that kept the towel safe, she shook her hair back and hurried across the bedroom.

Only it wasn't the housekeeper with cream for her hands. Marc stood outside. He too had showered and changed, and he was utterly overwhelming—a proud prince of darkness—with the leaping blue lights in those astonishing eyes the only sign of emotion in his handsome, ruthless face.

Heart jumping in her chest, Paige opened her mouth to say something—anything!—and seized gratefully on the arrival of Fancy, who demanded a pat.

Stooping, one hand on the knot between her breasts, Paige stroked the dog's head and tried to think of something sensible to say. 'Oh,' she murmured vaguely, 'she's still damp.'

'I've just washed the salt water out of her coat. Here's the cream I promised you for your hands.'

His voice was steady, almost deliberate, but the rasping note beneath the banal words tightened her every muscle, set every cell humming.

She straightened and without meeting his eyes said brightly, 'Thank you. My palms are starting to regret the last ten minutes in the dinghy.'

Marc held out the tube. With a foolish nod she took it, careful not to touch him. Tiny drums beat in her ears, and she resisted a strong urge to say his name and look at him.

Clumsily she stepped back, and tripped over Fancy, who'd sidled behind her to check out the bedroom. Paige cried out and time slid backwards, replaying itself in slow motion. Again she jerked sideways, this time trying to avoid falling on the dog.

Once again strong arms caught her. Once again she was turned into Marc's arms and looked up into eyes whose brilliant colour was being overwhelmed by darkness.

Paige's breath came fast and soft through her lips. Mutely she stared at him.

'This is getting to be a habit,' Marc said in a silky voice that sent the blood beating through her veins in a merciless tide.

'No,' she whispered, but whether it was an answer or a weak plea for him to let her go she didn't know, because her brain had turned to marshmallow the moment he touched her.

When his lips met hers it was like diving into the heart of the sun. Yet she tried to resist until her newborn love, reinforced by the bleak knowledge that after tomorrow she'd never see him again, flamed into a need so potent, so urgent, she surrendered to its insistent demand.

They kissed with a starving desperation that consumed her in a storm of sensation. Her hands stole up to clasp his neck and she opened her mouth and lost the last bit of herself in the taste, the scent of him, the heat from his body and his unleashed male power. Helplessly she responded to the rhythm of those kisses, falling further and further under the dark enchantment he wrought with his mouth and his touch.

She shuddered when he cupped her breast, shuddered

again when his thumb moved across the urgent nipple. Sensations so exquisitely fresh they were almost anguish sliced through her in sweet ferocity. At last she was going to find out what real desire was like—and she was fiercely glad that she had waited until she loved him before yielding.

She had no sexual tricks, no sophisticated techniques to offer him, and he didn't want her love, but this she could give—the untrained, honest responses of her body and her heart.

Yet he didn't know she was a virgin, and he might not value her gift. For a moment she froze, assailed by a chill of shyness.

'Paige. Look at me.'

The way he said her name and the kiss that accompanied it mixed desire and tenderness, as though he understood her fear.

She looked up, and he smiled and kissed her again, little kisses along her throat and across her shoulder, his mouth warm and seeking.

Her knees gave way; with a low, triumphant laugh he picked her up and lifted her high. Marvelling at the easy flexion of his body against hers, she looked up into his face. Passion emphasised the hawkish angles, gleamed darkly in his eyes, heated the skin across his sweeping cheekbones.

And then she remembered Juliette, and Lauren Porter. If she surrendered she'd be joining all those other women who'd loved Marc, only to discover that their love hadn't been enough for him.

He saw it happen. His expression hardened into distaste, the blue eyes glittering like frozen fire. 'You little tease,' he said, in a voice that blended savage anger and contempt, and set her down on her feet.

Humiliated, because her damned knees still wouldn't hold her upright, she had to grab his arm for support. But she found the strength to let him go and step back, although each movement weighed her down as though she was walking through quicksand.

'I take it that's a refusal,' he said with a slow, dangerously threatening smile.

She shook her head, feeling the heavy weight of her hair hot and tumbled on her neck. 'I'm not into fulfilling temporary needs,' she said huskily, despising herself for the bitter ache of grief.

His brow shot up, devastatingly ironic, but his voice was straight disdain. 'What do you want? A promise of permanence?'

'What would you know about permanence?' she asked in a low, scornful tone. 'Juliette wasn't enough for you, and even with Lauren Porter to cater to your every whim you're unable to keep faithful to her.'

White around the mouth, he surveyed her with hooded, molten eyes. 'Did Juliette tell you that?'

'Who else would?'

'She was wrong.' When she lifted her brows in disbelief he said with freezing distaste, 'Lauren and I are good and close friends, but there is nothing romantic or sexual between us.'

A wild tumult of emotions rocketed through her—a reckless desire to believe him, mixed with disgust and angry resentment. 'So why did Juliette think there was?'

'Like me, she grew up in a household where the husband couldn't keep his hands off other women.' He watched her with an unyielding expression. 'Unlike my mother, hers accepted her father's mistresses as a fact of life. Juliette grew up with a pragmatic outlook; she didn't believe in friendship between men and women. For her, there had to be a sexual component to any relationship.'

Horrified by the strength of her need to believe him, Paige remained obstinately silent.

He said harshly, 'I had no idea she saw Lauren as a threat until just before she was killed. I told her what I'm telling you—when I make vows I keep them. I was faithful to her.'

Paige couldn't formulate any answer. The hunger to believe him ate into her will power, but she didn't dare give in to it. Appalled, she realised that she was wringing her hands, and with an effort forced them apart to hang limply by her sides.

'Look at me,' he commanded.

Her hair swirled round her face as she shook her head.

'Paige, I don't believe this. You're such a valiant fighter I'd never have taken you for a coward.'

The note of amused gentleness in his voice shredded her determination. She glanced up and was lost, her gaze ensnared by the piercing brilliance of his.

He said roughly, 'I want you so much—so much—but not if you don't believe me. If there is nothing else between lovers, there must be truth.'

No man could speak with such blazing honesty and lie.

A shudder of need tightened her skin; she felt the small hard points of her breasts peak beneath the soft material of the bath sheet.

'Paige,' he said between his teeth, his voice so guttural she had difficulty discerning the words, 'turn around while I leave this room. Then lock your door after me.'

She'd intended to ask him whether Juliette had married him for practical reasons; she'd wanted to watch his face when he answered. But the idea fled as she met his eyes, points of sapphire flame in the golden skin of his sculpted face.

Longing and frustration combined like fire and petrol, urged on by an intensity of relief that Juliette had known the truth before she'd been so tragically taken; she said unevenly, 'Thank you for—I needed to know that. And I'm so glad Juliette didn't die believing that you had—that you were—'

He reached out to catch a tear slipping from the corner of her eye. In a hard voice he said, 'So am I. I don't deserve your tears, Paige, and she wouldn't have wanted you to cry for her.'

And as if he couldn't help it he lifted his hand and licked the tear from his finger. 'I have to go,' he said harshly. When she shook her head, he waited for a heart-stopping moment, then asked on a rough note, 'Are you certain, *mon coeur*?'

My heart—probably an everyday endearment in France, but she'd cherish the way he'd said it for the rest of her life.

'Yes.' She had never been more sure of anything in her life.

Her clamouring senses demanded satisfaction, but it was an upwelling of love that drove her to hold his hand against her cheek. Nothing, she realised with a swift, intense relief, had ever been more right than this. The last virginal tremors dissipated like dew under a benign sun as passion rioted through her, dazzling her with its stupendous intensity.

He turned and closed the door on Fancy. Then he pulled Paige gently against him and his mouth came down on her forehead.

'Are your arms and shoulders very painful?' he murmured.

Dimly she understood that he was giving her another chance to pull back. In some distant recess of her brain common sense drummed out warning and instructions, but she couldn't concentrate on anything but the clean, salty scent that was his alone. Essence of Marc, she thought desperately, fighting off the impulse to push her nose into his chest and inhale.

And his heat, curling around her like smoke, driving away the warnings until they turned into vapour and disappeared. Slowly, captured by the dilating intensity of his eyes, she slid her hand up to rest on his chest and luxuriated in his closeness.

Huskily, her mind finally surrendering to the barrage of sensory input, she said, 'My shoulders and arms are fine, but I think I can feel a chill coming on.'

His heart kicked against her palm. The heavy catch in its steady rhythm filled her with astonished triumph.

'We can't have that,' he said thickly, picking her up again and walking across the room.

Beside the bed she expected him to put her down, but instead he stopped and looked down into her face, his eyes almost black. Very quietly he asked, 'Are you sure you know what you're doing?'

Did he guess that this was the first time for her? She didn't care.

'Oh, yes,' she said huskily. And because she suspected that he was going to spell out that making love to her meant nothing beyond a momentary pleasure—a statement she wouldn't be able to bear—she lifted her head and kissed the words from his mouth.

When his arms tightened around her, and his demanding mouth turned that tentative kiss into an avowal of naked hunger, she accepted that she'd regret this surrender. Yet she knew she'd regret much more not making love with Marc.

And then she could no longer think. Banishing the last remnants of fear, she slipped the leash on her senses and allowed them to run riot.

Some time—a long time—later, her feet touched the floor. She swayed on boneless legs, dragging air into her famished lungs when he slid his hands beneath the towel and opened it. The damp bath sheet fell to the ground and she was exposed to him.

Swift colour stained her skin, turning it rose-gold. He was probably accustomed to women in silk and satin, she thought wildly, and wished she had some sexy, sensuous garment to wear.

He cupped a breast in his lean, strong hand. 'Look,' he said, his voice a deep rumble that reverberated through her.

She obeyed, sensation knotting in the pit of her stomach at the contrast of his long, tanned fingers against her gleaming skin.

'You're the colour of a peach,' he said quietly, and met her eyes with a stark urgency that splintered the last of her resistance.

All that mattered now was Marc, and her need to give him everything she could.

'Don't be shy,' he said, the slight French intonation in his voice strengthening. 'You are so beautiful, and I want you so much that I'm scared.'

'You?' she croaked as his thumb stroked the pleading nub of her breast with a skill that indicated his experience.

Sheer, astonishing pleasure shot from there to the rest of her body, scintillated across her nerves, lit up every cell in a parade of sensuous fireworks. Her breath choked in her lungs, then came and went swiftly through her parted lips.

He gave a soft, ironic laugh. 'Is that so surprising? Any man would be terrified by such beauty.' Before she could answer he buried his mouth in the hollow of her throat.

The touch of his lips fuelled her runaway anticipation, and when he nipped the spot where her neck joined her shoulder the sharp edges of his teeth produced an almost painful excitement.

She clung to him, gasping as he moved his hand upwards. For a moment she hung on the cusp between fear and violent anticipation, until he kissed her throat again and claimed her other breast with one teasing stroke of his fingers.

And then he said quietly, 'Take off my shirt.'

Her hands were shaking so much that she could barely push the buttons through their holes. When Marc shrugged free of the shirt she sighed, devouring him with shadowed eyes.

'You're so—so broad,' she breathed. Her fingertips lingered on smooth, hot, supple skin, sleekly taut over the hard swell of a muscle.

'I won't hurt you,' he said harshly.

She gave him a swift glance and looked away, her hand falling to her side. 'I know.'

And clearly he knew that she wasn't experienced. Was she being awkward and gauche? Should she explain that this was the first time for her—and run the risk of having him pull back?

No.

'How do you know that?' He caught her hand and rested it lightly against his chest, the soft abrasion of the pattern of hair a stimulus in itself.

She bit her lip. 'Pain is barbaric,' she murmured, 'and you're very civilised.'

He gave a bark of sardonic laughter. Paige looked up in surprise.

'At the moment,' he said, curving his hand around her breast, 'I'm very *un*civilised—almost purely primitive, in fact. But I won't hurt you.'

And he bent his black head and drew the tight, expectant nub of her breast into his mouth.

Paige froze, captured by impossible pleasure, by intolerable excitement. When he lifted his head she could have cried out in protest.

In a voice made deep and slow by carnal hunger, Marc said, 'Yes, you are beautiful, delicate and fragile as a flower, yet like a flower there's strength and determination in you.'

He picked her up and lowered her onto the bed. Still flushing, she watched with dilating eyes as he stripped. She was under no illusions; although she'd loved him for ever, and he wanted her now, his desire was deceptive and illusory as moonshine, a fleeting, beautiful thing. She would make love with him, and when it was time she'd leave with her pride intact and without a backward glance.

With slow, drugging expertise Marc kissed every thought from her head, and when he lifted his mouth he was beside her on the bed, an arm around her shoulders holding her against his lean, eager body.

A primal thrill scorched through Paige. Somewhere outside a gull screeched, its angry, spiteful call jaggedly reminding her that there was a reality outside the room and this man.

She didn't care.

Turning her head, she kissed his shoulder, then licked where she'd kissed; the faint salty taste of his skin was fiercely erotic to her, as was the tight sound from his throat and the dark flames in his eyes.

He ran a hand down her body, beginning at her throat and finishing at the place where her thighs met, and while her lashes slowly fluttered down he gave a crooked smile and began to show her exactly what magic a man and a woman could make together.

The instinct that had warned her he'd be a consummate lover had been dead on target. Marc seemed to understand more about her body than she did. He knew that his mouth on her breast twisted sensation inside her, tightening it until she sobbed on a shivering wave of heated rapture.

He explored her with his mouth, unlocking a reckless response that built and built and built until she was sobbing with a delicious frustration, her hands clenched by her sides and her body a taut, pleading bow under his ministrations.

Eventually she whispered in a hoarse, desperate little voice, 'Please. Marc, I can't—I want—'

His kiss pressed her head back into the pillow with its depth and demand, and while she was lost in that sorcery he moved over her, prolonging the kiss as he eased into her.

A sharp jab brought Paige's eyelashes bolting up. Dazedly she stared into Marc's eyes and read astonishment there, and then—amazingly—a white-hot satisfaction.

Harshly he said, 'I'm sorry—I didn't know.'

'It's all right,' she said, desperation cutting across the words as the ardent delight receded a little.

He kissed her again, and against her lips he murmured, 'Try to relax.'

'I can't,' she said, starkly honest, her hands gripping his shoulders. 'I want you too much.'

'So?' The muscles beneath her hands bunched and he pushed, slowly widening that path until the fragile barrier ripped.

Urgently she said, 'It's not—it's fine.'

'Good.' And he drove home.

What followed was pure drama. Never losing control, he wooed her with his body and his voice, driving her further and further up the sides of some insurmountable cliff, a long, pleasure-drenched journey where he was guide and mentor. At last, poised on the brink of rapturous knowledge, she reached the top and spun off into delight, ecstatic waves breaking through her body until she could bear it no longer.

Almost immediately he followed her, big body taut as a bow, and without realising it made her his for all time.

Her last thought, barely coherent before she slipped into sleep, was that whatever happened to her in the future she had this memory of delight to treasure.

It was dusk when she woke, with the distant noise of a helicopter buzzing in her ears. She turned towards the empty side of the bed, unconsciously questing, then re-membered, and blushed, and lay for several moments while the memories flooded through her.

Stretching luxuriously, she thought that no other woman in the world could have had such a long, idyllically sensual introduction to making love. Marc had been gentle and skilful, until gentleness and skill had been abandoned in raw male fire as desire overtook him.

It had been perfect. Marc had been perfect. She thought idly that she was no longer a virgin, and smiled, enjoying the tiny signals of his possession—her tender lips, a small ache between her legs, the deep, lingering sensuality.

Loving Marc had opened her to change, shown her that if this once was all she'd ever have of him—well, it would be enough for a lifetime. Because after this there would be no other man for her.

But she knew now that she wouldn't retreat from life as

her mother had; instead, she'd live it richly and fully, because love meant much more than a cowardly dependence.

She moved restlessly on the bed, turning to look at the indentation on the pillow beside her where Marc's head had rested. Satiety bred appetite; instead of being satisfied with the miracle he'd made for her she wanted to loosen the bars on the wild need that sang in forbidden cadences through her body, demanding a like response from him too.

She wanted him to lose control as she had lost it; she wanted him to know the almost aggressive craving that felt as though it might tear her apart—to feel it and to be forced to surrender to it.

'It isn't going to happen,' she said aloud. 'So take what you got and be contented.'

If she made love with him again it would shatter her self-esteem and break her heart. Marc might have ravished her soul from her body, but neither that afternoon or now had he said anything about a future.

So she'd have to resist this intense love that undermined every warning, every sensible thought and decision.

'Why?' she asked suddenly. After all, she'd made love to him knowing that he wasn't going to offer her permanence—he'd made sure of that with brutal frankness.

Resisting him would be cutting off her nose to spite her face.

She had tonight—their last night together. And, because she wasn't wasting a moment of it, she sprang out of bed and into the shower, then dressed swiftly before going out to see where he was.

Marc looked up from his desk. His eyes narrowed when he saw Paige wander across the lawn towards the beach.

She looked forlorn, he thought, and found himself on his feet, setting off to make everything better for her.

Fortunately logic kicked in before he'd taken more than a couple of steps. His mouth compressed into a straight line and he strode back to his desk, stepping over a co-matose Fancy.

This desire to smooth the way for her was suspicious. He swore beneath his breath; he'd assumed that at her age she'd have had some experience. Her virginity had sur-prised the hell out of him.

And pleased him far too much, he thought with a twist of self-derision. He hadn't ever made love to a virgin be-fore and, damn it, it changed things.

So what to do now?

The telephone rang. Impatiently he picked it up and barked, 'Yes?'

'Darling, I'll be with you in an hour,' Lauren said, not at all discomposed. 'I've got everything ready; there's just a couple of things to finalise, papers for you to sign off, and then it will be done. See you soon.'

Marc put the telephone down and frowned, his eyes on the solitary figure walking along the beach. Fancy had gone out to join her and they made a pretty picture in the dying glow of the sun, outlined in a crimson glow against the shimmer of the sea.

Closing down the computer took a couple of seconds while he sorted the papers he'd need later that night, when he spoke to his office in London.

Then he went out into the soft spring dusk, scented with the sea and the perfume of the season, a sensuous breath of growth and fertility. His mouth quirked cynically when he noted a glow behind the hill that promised a full moon. A cliché if ever there was one!

Yet clichés had power, and in spite of himself his instincts woke, strong and powerfully primal within him. But not tonight, he thought. For too many reasons; Lauren would be here, and Paige would be...

She'd gone down to the edge of the water and was standing very still as she stared out to sea, her slender body held upright by that steel spine.

As he watched she straightened already straight shoulders and stooped to pick up a stone, hurling it across the water.

It skipped five times before sinking.

'You've practised that,' Marc said drily, walking down to join her.

Paige's heart jumped. Sheer force of will stopped her from whirling around, but her voice sounded breathy and startled when she said, 'For about three months when I was ten.'

'It must be a ten-year-old's rite of passage.' He strolled down onto the sand, Fancy a silent shadow at his heels. 'My father taught me how to do it here.'

He stooped, picked up a flat, round pebble and sent it out with a deft twist of his wrist. Both watched it skip six times before falling into the water.

'Do you take everything so competitively?' Paige asked wryly.

He shrugged. 'I wasn't trying to beat your score, but competition was bred into me.'

He kept so much of himself hidden that Paige held her breath, wondering if she dared follow up this tiny hint. What had his father been like? Had he shown his son a softer side?

'No quarter given?' she asked.

'He played to win, even when I was four and he was teaching me chess.'

Her heart twisted at the thought of a small boy faced

with his father's determination to beat him. 'I'll bet he was a bad loser.'

He laughed. 'The first time I got him he admitted defeat with gritted teeth, but I heard him bragging about it to a friend. He was proud of me.'

'Ah,' she said softly, 'one of those supreme moments, like the instant you realise that it's you, not the bike, in control.'

There was amusement in his voice when he agreed, yet through the comfortable silence that followed a familiar wild hunger simmered through her veins.

She gestured at the crimson afterglow of the sunset over the mainland and said, 'I can see why you call this place home. It's completely, ravishingly beautiful.'

And she'd eat her heart out for it—and its owner—after she left.

'Beauty beyond compare,' he agreed, turning his head so that for a moment the crimson light from the sea was reflected onto his profile. His beautiful mouth sketched an ironic smile. 'But if we don't want to see a very stern Rose Oliver we'd better get inside and think about a drink before dinner.'

It was a definite closing of the door that had so temporarily opened. Paige flinched internally, but turned with him and went across the lawn and into the house.

'I'll change,' she said quietly.

As she got into a simple straight skirt and a sleeveless scoop-necked top in a soft bronze that gave a deeper glow to her hair, she heard a helicopter fly in, fast and low, its rotors thumping as it landed on the pad.

Bringing someone? She stopped combing her hair and bit her lip, but she had no right to complain.

Yet outside the door to the morning room she stopped and gathered her courage in both her hands. Through it she could hear voices, so, yes, someone had arrived. And she was almost sure she knew who it was.

Her skin chilled, and she opened the door.

Marc and Lauren were looking out of the window at the sunset. Although they weren't touching, something about the silence that encompassed them clamped every muscle in Paige's body into punishing rigidity.

Anguish stabbed her in a region of her heart she hadn't known existed. He had lied, she thought painfully; *this* was how Juliette had known they were lovers. Their intimacy was so obvious it blazed as brightly as Marc's eyes.

She hadn't expected commitment, but she had believed him when he'd said he and Lauren weren't lovers—only to be betrayed. And he'd betrayed Lauren too.

Did any man keep his promises?

Forced to watch as Lauren looked into Marc's face and laughed, she recognised love in that soft sound—and a teasing inflection that hurt even more because it spoke of knowledge and equality.

'Oh, Marc,' his lover said, 'you darling idiot!'

CHAPTER ELEVEN

BEYOND thought, acting on a desperate instinct to protect herself from utter humiliation, Paige made a production of closing the door behind her. When she turned back to the room both Marc and Lauren had swung around.

Side by side, the link between them blazed as obvious as the posters at the strip club. A slow anger began to boil inside her as she saw them focus their attention onto her, deliberately concealing that silent, intangible connection.

Whipping up the remnants of shattered pride to stiffen her spine, Paige went towards them, her head held high enough to strain her shoulders and neck.

His handsome face impassive, Marc said, 'What would you like to drink before dinner, Paige? There's wine and sherry, or orange juice if you'd rather.'

Paige would much rather. Anything alcoholic might loosen the fierce leash she'd clamped on her emotions. Forcing herself to overcome an anguish so strong she could barely breathe, she said, 'I'd love orange juice, thank you,' wondering if she sounded as stilted to them as she did in her own ears.

Marc glanced at the woman beside him. 'Lauren? The usual?'

'Thank you.' She smiled at Paige—a warm smile that hurt its recipient more than anything else since she'd come into the room.

She could see why, in spite of everything, Juliette had liked this woman.

Who said now, 'How lucky you are to live in Hawke

Bay. When I'm in New Zealand I always like to try your superb wines, especially the *sauvignon blanc* and *pinot gris*. And your winemakers are producing some excellent reds.'

She had what sounded like an impeccable French accent. As well as wine, she'd probably be able to eloquently discuss food and the latest books and shows.

If Paige's smile was as ragged as it felt on her lips, neither seemed to notice. 'Living in a wine-growing district means that I've absorbed information by osmosis, but I have to admit I don't know much about it.' Grateful for the steadiness of her voice, she added, 'When it comes to discussing the finer points of New Zealand styles and vintages I'm lost.'

But after Marc had given them their respective drinks he began to talk of Northland's new boutique wineries. Paige didn't have to feign attention; he had the rare ability of being able to invest any subject with interest.

And even knowing that he's lied to you and betrayed you you'd listen to him for the pleasure of hearing his voice, an inner demon jeered.

Cynicism was good; it stopped her from remembering how it had felt to be in his arms, to—

Ruthlessly she dragged her mind back to the conversation, which had moved onto new industries in New Zealand's northernmost province. Northland's long, slender peninsula, pointing to the tropics, had traditionally been an agricultural and holiday area, but this was changing, and from what he and Lauren said Marc was a major player in that change.

Paige found that she could cope if she pretended she was acting in a play—as the foil for the main characters, she thought bitterly. Every second since she'd walked in had reinforced the bond between them; they knew each other very, very well.

By the time the housekeeper called them for dinner her throat had tightened, and after a couple of surreptitious swallows she knew she wasn't going to be able to eat.

Yet to save face she'd have to force food past the hard, heavy lump in her chest. A judicious lubrication of wine might help; she nodded when Marc offered a glass of red, and when it was poured took a slow, cautious sip.

'Do you like that?' he asked, startling her.

She looked no further than his chin. 'It's delicious,' she said politely.

'Tell me what you taste when you drink it.'

'Is this some kind of test?' she asked, her tone a little too sweet.

Lauren made a soft noise that could have been a stifled laugh.

Long fingers relaxed around the base of his glass, Marc leaned back and looked across the table. Candlelight flickered sensuously across his dark face, accenting the hawk-like features. Paige's stomach clenched into a knot and her spine went into instant meltdown.

I have to get away before I make a total fool of myself, she thought feverishly.

'I'm interested in your opinion,' he said mildly, yet a steely note ran through the words and his hard, blue gaze didn't leave her face.

She shrugged. 'It's—well, the word that comes to mind is earthy—yet I think I can taste plums. And a hint of liquorice.' She hesitated before adding with a touch of defiance that hid, she hoped, her wounded outrage, 'All in all, an arrogant vintage with hidden depths.'

Lauren's laughter broke the silence. 'She got you there, Marc. As clever a piece of subtext as I've come across in a while.'

One raised black brow indicated Marc's mocking amusement. 'You have a palate.'

Shamefully flattered, Paige said stiffly, 'Doesn't everyone?'

'Not as naturally sensitive as yours.'

When he smiled at her it was hard to remember that this was the man who'd lied to her, then seduced her, even though he must have known his mistress was arriving later that day.

She glanced at Lauren, caught an odd little smile curling her perfect mouth, and decided she was either depraved or she didn't know what sort of man she loved.

Paige called on every ounce of composure she possessed to say, 'How gratifying.'

'Another accomplishment to add to your list,' he said urbanely.

The note of irony in his words told her he'd recognised her withdrawal. Heat stung her skin. What did he mean by that?

Staring at the food on her plate with dogged determination, Paige responded, 'A good sense of taste is hardly an accomplishment.'

'And that's a reply that shows a charming humility.' Marc's dry voice altered, becoming infused with a coolly goading irony that stopped Paige's heart. 'You should be proud of your many and varied talents.'

Surely he wouldn't mention those frenzied hours in his arms—not in front of the woman who was listening with every appearance of composure—even, she thought on a spark of anger, *amusement*—to this conversation.

There was a deadly little silence before he finished, 'Lauren has been remarking on your sense of style, and Sherry told me you have green fingers.'

The glimmer of the candlelight hid any expression in

his eyes. And was that a sleekly patronising smile from the high-powered executive beside him?

Paige refused to respond with anything other than a wooden, 'Thank you,' and when Lauren stepped in with an innocuous comment about gardening she could only summon a resentful gratitude.

She chewed grimly and made herself swallow even when her stomach showed signs of rebelling. And she made stilted conversation about her interest in plants.

'A friend of mine breeds roses,' Marc said deliberately. 'You might have heard of him—Adam Curwen.'

Her gaze, pure green in the subdued light, crossed swords with his. 'He's brilliant,' she said thinly. 'A trendsetter, yet his roses are tough and healthy and their scent is glorious.'

'I'll introduce him to you one day. He'd be—'

Rain drowned his voice—sudden, tempestuous pellets slashing onto the roof and across the windows. Paige noted the way one of Lauren's brows shot up as she sent a swift glance at Marc.

In spite of everything she could do to quench it a tiny fugitive flame of hope flickered into life in the cold region of her heart. He'd spoken as though there was some sort of future for them...

No, she thought fiercely. She wasn't like Juliette or Lauren—she wouldn't share him. It was demeaning and humiliating; it would be a slow death of the things that mattered most—her integrity, her self-respect.

If she couldn't be the only woman in his life she'd rather not have him in hers. Sometimes the price of love came too high.

When the fusillade of rain had passed, Lauren said sympathetically, 'It's a pity it's been so wet while you're here.'

Carefully avoiding Marc's eyes, Paige smiled. 'Actually,

it's been lovely in between the showers, and I expected the rain—Northland is notorious for its humidity.'

'Spoken like a loyal daughter of Hawke Bay's drier, more Mediterranean climate,' Marc said. He paused for a second, then added in an aloof tone underlined with a subtle taunt, 'Rain has its benefits—lush fertility, and an abundance of natural beauty.'

Light collected in his wine as he raised the glass to his mouth, then flashed crimson when he drank. Paige felt her colour deepen, and because her hand quivered she set her fork down with a sharp little crash that seemed to reverberate around the room.

She wondered if she was being absurdly sensitive. It was ridiculous to suspect an underlying meaning in everything he said!

Lauren murmured, 'But all of New Zealand—all that I've seen, anyway—is beautiful. Even your cities are set in glorious surroundings.'

'We're very lucky,' Paige agreed, welcoming the change of subject with galling relief. 'Of the cities you've visited, which one did you enjoy the most?'

'Paris,' Lauren said promptly, with a wistful smile that made her seem more vulnerable. She was silent a moment. 'But there are so many wonderful places in the world—and I hate to think that in one lifetime I'm never going to get around them all!'

And she talked charmingly of some of her favourites.

Later, as Paige prepared for bed, she prayed she'd been able to hide her turbulent emotions. She thought she'd managed to behave like an adult—one who'd never touched Marc, never kissed him, never lain with him in this bed and given him everything she had.

After dinner he'd asked courteously if she wanted to

watch a film. Equally courteous, she'd told him that she was a little tired so she'd go to bed.

He had got to his feet. 'How are your shoulders?'

'Just a bit stiff.'

'Shower before you go to bed and let the water play on your back again,' he'd advised.

'I'll do that,' she'd told him colourlessly.

Only twelve hours of this farce to go, she had reminded herself as she'd smiled meaninglessly in their general direction and turned towards the door.

Now, sitting on her bed, she wondered how on earth she was going to get through the night.

A bitter, aching sense of loss submerged her. And that was stupid, because how could she lose what she'd never had? Her involuntary, electric awareness of him—even her reluctant love—seemed indecent now she'd seen that invisible, undeniable bond between Marc and Lauren. But worse was the corroding jealousy that came dangerously near resentment.

'Brooding isn't going to help.' She climbed to her feet with the effort of someone determined not to give in to pain, and went into the opulent, scented bathroom.

And she was not going to surrender to self-pity. She'd find the guts and determination to make something of her life. Marc's sexual initiation of her might have been without the emotion she craved from him, but he'd given her a rare and precious gift—knowledge of her own sensuality and complete satisfaction.

Gripping the counter, she stared at herself in the mirror, meeting eyes tormented by secrets above a mouth with fuller, more ardent contours than she'd seen before.

In Marc's arms she'd crossed the perilous border from inexperience to knowledge.

'You already know that life can be tough—learn to deal with it,' she advised tautly.

She had to, because after the next day she was never going to see him again.

Grimacing, she fought back another wave of pain. She'd been such an idiot—so eager to co-operate in her own undoing, willingly tricking herself into believing that making love to Marc would mean something to him, even when he'd told her it wouldn't.

At least he'd made sure that there would be no unwanted results from their loving. She blinked hard, because now she knew why Sherry was so determined to do the best for Brodie; she too would have protected Marc's child, no matter what she had to do.

She tried hard to feel thankful that it wasn't going to happen.

Unbidden, a thought clawed its way through the tumult in her brain. Perhaps the closeness between Lauren and him was the rapport of ex-lovers who were now friends?

Her heart leapt, but Paige had done enough wishful thinking that day to learn her lesson. 'No,' she said with scornful contempt.

There had been real affection in their attitude to each other, a kind of unspoken empathy they didn't notice because it was so familiar.

Was Lauren like Juliette, sweetly complaisant and docile, content with the sort of relationship that gave Marc freedom to do what he wanted when he wanted with any other woman he wanted?

'She might be, but I'm not,' Paige said grimly. In the mirror she saw anger contort her face, and thought painfully, I can't bear this. I'm turning into a different person and I hate it. It's better to find out now that I'll never be able to trust him.

But oh, it *hurt*.

Back in Napier, away from his disturbing effect on her, she'd pick up the shards of her life and cement them back together; she'd find a job that had something to do with her interests. Certainly she'd opt out of the battle between the sexes. Love was a war zone, with far more losers than winners.

Until tomorrow she had to grit her teeth, keep reminding herself of the sort of man Marc was, and endure.

Although the prospect of life without him crumbled something strong and vital in her, she'd cope. Time was on her side, because she was stronger than her mother— she wasn't going to waste her life yearning for a man she couldn't trust.

Yet as she got into the shower she knew that some part of her would never recover; oh, she'd manage, but for her there would be no other man—she'd go to her grave wanting Marc.

'Don't be so melodramatic,' she scoffed.

Safely camouflaged by the rush of water, she let the tears fall, giving in—just this once—to the grief sifting through her soul like a grey mist.

Once in bed she kept her restless mind busy by working out vicious ways of paying Marc back. For what? she mocked. Making her want him? Making her lose her head? He hadn't even tried; she'd fallen headlong and with insulting ease.

But anger gave her strength, whereas desolation leached it away. And right now she needed strength.

And she was not in love with him! If you loved someone you were supposed to want their happiness above all else.

What she wanted above all else was to get away from Marc and lick her wounds and remake her life...

After what seemed hours of tossing in the bed she

opened her eyes, blinking at the hard, white slabs of moonlight that fell through the shutters and tiger-striped the floor.

She switched on her light and peered at the bedside clock.

She'd been in bed under thirty minutes. It was, she thought, her bravado fading under a wave of weary misery, going to be a long night.

'Yeah, that's good. You're getting the hang of it. That graft'll take.'

Paige flushed. The elderly nurseryman was sparing with his praise so this was a rare moment.

They stood for a couple of moments evaluating the rose bush before he remarked, 'I don't know why you're so set on going to university—it's a waste of time. Breeding new plants is mostly knowing what they want, and you get that by growing them. After that it's gut feelings and persistence and a good eye. I reckon you've got those already.'

Paige too had been wondering whether the money Juliette had left her would be wasted on university fees. 'I don't have to make a decision for a couple of months.'

'Well, you're doing pretty good. Don't forget to clean that grafting knife.'

'I won't.'

He strode off, then turned. 'Knew I came out here for something. There's a joker out front wants to talk to you.'

During the past three months Paige had thought she'd blocked out the fantasy that Marc might walk back into her life, but there it was again, painfully sharp and instant. Stop it now, she thought, putting the grafting knife down. It's not going to happen.

She was knitting her life together with dreams and will power, and she wasn't going to let a stupid obsession ruin her progress.

'Who is it?' she asked casually.

'Never seen him before.'

She glanced at her watch. 'I'm not expecting anyone. He can wait until finishing time.'

'Ten minutes won't do him any harm,' her boss agreed. 'But you worked all through lunchtime so you might as well go now.'

It took her ten minutes to wash her hands and take off her overalls, then run a comb through her hair without scanning her face. She knew what she'd see there—opaque eyes, a mouth that had somehow tightened over the past three months, a general air of tense control.

It was hot in the cloakroom; she pulled her T-shirt away from her body and puffed out her cheeks. She had a long ride home.

Small pack on her back, she wheeled her bicycle around the shabby building, part office, part greenhouse, then stopped in the shade of a huge silk tree. Dismay hammered at her—dismay and a wild exhilaration that broke through the crust of ice she'd moulded around her emotions. Only one man in her acquaintance would be driving a car like this expensive European saloon.

Marc had seen her coming. The car door opened and he got out, wearing strength and power with a formidable authority that reinforced his height and the spread of his shoulders.

'Paige,' he said with uncompromising self-possession, scrutinising her. 'How are you?'

Dry-mouthed, she returned, 'Stunned.' And grubby and angry, she told herself fiercely. It had to be anger that drove the colour into her skin and stirred up her energy levels, sending blood racing through her body.

That satirical eyebrow shot up and he smiled narrowly. 'Stunned? I'm surprised—surely you didn't expect your coldly formal farewell at Kerikeri airport to be the final words between us?'

She was staring at him as though he'd walked out of a spaceship and demanded to be taken to her leader. It was, Marc thought with cold self-derision, patently obvious she hadn't been expecting him. He knew why, too; all the men in her life had abandoned her in their various ways.

As he had.

Damn, she'd lost weight since he'd put her on the plane. Her face was more finely drawn; perhaps the heat and working two jobs were grinding her down. But her mouth still beckoned with lushly sensuous impact, and he still wanted her as much as he had before.

More.

'I think we've said everything there is to say to each other,' she retorted, not giving an inch, her square jaw lifting a fraction and her eyes gleaming green.

'Do you?' He held her gaze until the thick black lashes swept down and her colour faded.

'Yes,' she said coldly, hating him for doing this to her. 'And I'm afraid I'm running late, so I have to go.'

'I'll give you a ride home.'

'No, thank you.' She sent a savage, meaningless smile in his direction. 'I need my bike to get me here tomorrow morning.'

'You work on Sundays?'

Feeling like a total idiot for forgetting that today was Saturday, she held his eyes steadily. 'On Monday, then.'

'Your bike will go in the boot.'

Her laughter lacked humour. 'It will also scratch the paint.'

She stiffened at his negligent shrug, and the anger that was holding her upright intensified into cold rage when he said indifferently, 'So?'

'So I don't want a lift home.'

'I need to talk to you—'

'What about what *I* need?' she demanded.

Coolly arrogant, he returned, 'You need it too.'

'Like a hole in the head,' she said inelegantly, adding with rigid disdain, 'If it's my welfare you're interested in, as you can see I'm fine. I'm thoroughly enjoying working here, and learning a lot.' She dragged in a swift, shallow breath and hurtled on, 'Sherry and Brodie are settled and well. She loves her employers; they love her. She adores living in the country and she's switched from saving every cent she can for the deposit on a house to investing in stocks and shares.'

'The share market had better watch out,' he said with a lazy smile that scorched the length of her spine. 'Are you pregnant?'

Her fingers clenched on the handlebars. Well, of course! She should have thought of that. In spite of the precautions he'd taken, Marc Corbett covered all bases; he wouldn't want an inconvenient child on the periphery of his life!

Fighting back a buzzing in her head, she said baldly, 'No.'

'You're sure of that?'

She met his assessing eyes with a fiercely independent glare. 'Absolutely one hundred per cent sure. But even if I were, what would you do about it?'

'Marry you,' he said grimly.

Astonishment widened her eyes, but she made a swift recovery. 'Not even you,' she said, the metal in her words as cutting as steel, 'can do the impossible. I wouldn't marry you if I were pregnant, but it isn't relevant because I'm not. Now, go back to your world and leave me in mine.'

He reached her before she had time to swing her leg

over the bicycle. Strong hands closed over the handlebars and stopped the machine from moving.

'Once you asked me if Juliette had been happy. Now I'm asking you—are you happy?' he asked, his voice aloof.

But when she looked up she read an iron, uncompromising will in the hard angles and planes of his face.

She folded her lips together firmly and met his scrutiny with defiance that covered, she prayed, the pain beneath. 'Let my bike go, please,' she said between her teeth.

'I'd like to explain some things to you.'

'I can't talk to you. I have to get home because I go to another job, and I'm due there in an hour.' She hated lying to him, but she had to get out of here—his closeness was melting her resolve like a blowtorch on ice.

Her father's rejection had scarred her life and coloured her attitudes. Without realising it, she'd organised her life so that no man could get close enough to her to spurn her love. Somehow she'd twisted her feelings so much she'd even welcomed Marc's statement that he wasn't offering anything but sex because it freed her from her fear of rejection.

But she could no longer lie to herself. In spite of everything, she loved him, and every moment she spent with him brought her closer to admitting it.

'Coming home with me will make up time,' he said crisply. 'Get in—I'll put this in the boot.'

Mind racing, she hesitated; a seething glance told her he wasn't going to move, and short of yelling for help she had no chance of getting away. And perhaps this talk he wanted would give her an ending, a way to finally cut him out of her heart.

'Is this how you got to be a tycoon?' she asked scornfully. 'By nagging and harassment?'

He lifted the bike and dumped it in the car's big boot, lowering the top carefully to avoid scratching the gleaming paint. 'I prefer to call it bloody-minded perseverance,' he told her gravely.

Once they were purring down the road she asked, 'What is so important that it brings you here again?'

'I'll wait until we get home,' he said with infuriating self-possession. 'Tell me what you've been doing.'

Almost she snarled, but it wouldn't do any good, so she unclenched her jaw and kept her eyes on the road ahead. 'Working,' she returned steadily. 'And playing with Brodie when Sherry comes into town. He's grown such a lot—he can sit up and make noises, and laugh.' With the slightest of snaps she said, 'How's Lauren?'

'She's fine, and sends her regards.'

'Oh.' Disconcerted, Paige sent a sideways glance at him, and met eyes the polished blue of a gun barrel.

Her stomach jolting into free-fall, she turned her gaze ahead again.

Marc asked, 'Why are you working two jobs?'

Shrugging, she said, 'I need to earn as much as I can before the start of the next academic year.'

'So what sort of job takes up your Saturday night?'

'Oh, of course. Today's Saturday,' she said lamely. 'Ah, during the week I clean offices.' Ashamed, she stared out of the side window.

He didn't say anything, for which she was grateful. She should have known better than to lie; her mother had used to tell her she was the world's worst fibber.

CHAPTER TWELVE

BACK at the unit, Paige turned and fixed her gaze just past Marc's ear. 'I'm grubby. I need to shower and change.'

'I'll make you coffee.' Marc looked across at the kitchen and observed with irritating blandness, 'I'm glad to see you're using the electric jug I bought.'

'I don't cut off my nose to spite my face,' she said shortly, and disappeared.

After showering in record time, she changed into clean jeans and a dark green T-shirt. For the first time since she'd left Arohanui, she realised with a sinking feeling in her stomach, she looked human again. Sparks of gold glittered in her green eyes, her cheeks were pink, and her heart pumped blood so vigorously through her system that she felt alert and vital and ready for anything.

But when Marc left she'd be right back where she started—desolated and wretched.

So? She could cope, even if it took every ounce of will power she possessed.

She set her chin at a jaunty angle and walked into her tiny living room.

Marc's glance registered nothing more dangerous than cool assessment. Handing her a mug of coffee, he said abruptly, 'When I told you I was faithful to Juliette, I was lying.'

'I know.' She tried to hide her raw, exposed emotions with an expressionless voice.

A muscle flicked in his arrogant jaw. 'You don't know why.'

Paige bit back the scornful words that threatened to spill out and waited in an agony of apprehension for him to tell her that he loved Lauren.

He said levelly, 'When I met you, I looked at you and I wanted you—the classic *coup de foudre*.'

Bewildered, she stared at his harshly angular face. 'I don't—'

'Thunderbolt,' he translated with bleak brevity. 'And, like a thunderbolt, it scared the hell out of me. And it wasn't one-sided. Don't shake your head—do you think I don't recognise when a woman wants me, even a seventeen-year-old virgin who doesn't know what the hell has happened to her? You did your best to resist it, and you succeeded in hiding it from anyone else, but I knew—and was infuriated and humiliated, because there was nothing more to it than mindless, elemental hunger.'

'I—yes, I know,' she said inaudibly, bracing herself.

Whatever she'd expected, it wasn't this. He was going to tell her that he'd been exorcising an old obsession when they'd made love.

The thought made her sick. Get on with it, she told him silently. Just do what it is you need to do and then go! Clenching her teeth together, she stared into the depths of her coffee and watched the liquid swirl lazily around.

Tonelessly he said, 'So I ignored it. I had made a promise to Juliette and I kept it.' He paused, before continuing in a tone laced with self-disgust, 'But I couldn't forget you. I carried you like a shining talisman, a memento of something precious that never happened, in my head and in my heart. I don't know whether Juliette sensed that, but I suspect it was what convinced her that Lauren was my mistress.'

Coffee slopped over the side of her mug. Ignoring it, Paige whispered, 'Oh, *no*!'

'She never knew,' he said swiftly, taking the mug from her and setting it down on the table. 'She valued your friendship highly. From the start we both understood that ours was a practical marriage. She wasn't in love with me and she knew I wasn't in love with her. I liked her very much, and I was sure I could make her happy. It never occurred to me she'd decide that Lauren and I were having an affair.'

'How could she not?' Paige still didn't believe him, although something niggled at the back of her mind. She added trenchantly, 'When I saw you and Lauren together there was such a sense of—of love and trust—and a deep, deep connection that can't be mistaken. If she's not your lover, what *is* she?'

He didn't answer straight away. Paige couldn't look at him; in an agony of suspense she waited, listening to her heart thud noisily in her throat.

Without inflection he said, 'I must ask you to keep this confidential, although I have her permission to tell you. She's my half-sister.'

Paige's jaw dropped. Incredulously, she repeated, 'Your *half-sister*!'

That small muscle flicked again in his jaw. 'Her mother and my father had an affair—one of his many affairs—and Lauren was the result.' He spoke austerely, his body language indicating his contempt. 'She doesn't want anyone to know because her parents are still alive and her father believes she is his child—as she is in everything but genetic heritage. She loves him, and he has a weak heart. She's worried that if he ever found out not only would it wreck her parents' marriage but it could kill her father.'

Stunned, Paige picked up her coffee mug and took a fortifying sip. All she could think of to say was a feeble, 'How did she learn about it?'

'A medical emergency when she was twenty-two—I donated bone marrow.'

'But surely her father realised then—?'

His mouth twisted. 'Her mother was desperate and contacted me, hoping I might be a compatible donor. Fortunately I was; apparently she told her husband that I was on the worldwide register. She asked me not to tell anyone. So I didn't—not even Juliette. But I was determined to keep in touch with Lauren; when she asked if she could join the firm I agreed. She is extremely good at her work, and utterly loyal.'

'I'm not surprised; you saved her life. I don't know how I missed it, but you have the same bone structure,' Paige said quietly, wondering now at her own blindness. It was too early, and too presumptuous, to be relieved. 'And you both lift your left eyebrow; I noticed that, but not anything else except that special rapport between you.'

'Juliette never saw the physical resemblance,' Marc said remotely, his lashes hiding all but narrow slivers of blue.

Paige's fingers twisted together. 'But she knew that there was something not right about your marriage. I feel that I betrayed her.'

He stared at her as though she was crazy. She expected an explosion, and for a moment she thought she was going to get one, but eventually he closed his eyes and dragged in a breath. When he opened his eyes and expelled the air from his lungs he'd re-established control.

'How?' he asked, almost temperately.

'If you kept on wanting me, even when you were married to her—' She stopped, because so much had been unsaid.

His brows drew together. 'Go on.'

The words tied themselves in knots on her tongue, but

she had to keep going. 'I can't bear to think I made her unhappy.'

He exhaled again, and ran a hand through his black hair. 'If anyone made her unhappy,' he pointed out in a tone that strove for reason, 'I did. You were totally innocent.'

She bit her lip. 'I wanted you.'

'Paige, stop staring at me as though I'm the enemy.' He strode across to the door and stared for a moment outside, as though working out what to say next. After a charged moment he swung around. 'Sit down. You look as though you've been run over by a Jumbo Jet.'

Reluctantly she obeyed, crossing her legs at the ankle, setting the mug on the table and then locking her nervous fingers together in her lap.

'I need to tell you about my marriage, and to do that I have to tell you about my family,' he said in a crisp, unemotional voice. 'To begin with, my father was notorious for his affairs.'

Paige realised he was hating this. She asked soberly, 'Is that why they called him the Robber Baron?'

He paused. 'Only partly. He conducted business like one of the old robber barons of industry. He always vowed he loved my mother—and I think in a strange sort of way he did.'

Paige snorted, and he smiled without humour. 'I couldn't agree more. My mother loved him desperately. She couldn't cope with his amours, and he didn't seem to be able to stop himself. Not that he was a rake; he chose sophisticated women, not innocents. I think I told you once that my childhood was punctuated by hideous rows and even more hideous silences; what I didn't tell you was that there were at least three suicide attempts by my mother. There may have been more.'

Paige made a shocked, sympathetic noise. Outside, the sun blazed down, silhouetting him against its brazen light.

Still in that toneless voice he said, 'I decided that I wouldn't ever put a woman through that; I wanted no part of love. I wanted a sensible marriage, where both of us knew exactly where we stood.'

'I can see why,' she admitted, horrified. Her own father's behaviour was nothing compared to this—at least he'd stayed with his second wife until he died.

'I chose Juliette because she loved children, she knew her way around the world I live in, and she was intelligent and kind. And she was beautiful—going to bed with her would be a pleasure.'

Outraged, Paige snapped, 'It sounds as though you made a list!'

His mouth tightened. 'And because although she liked me, and found me sexy and interesting, she wasn't in love with me. You noticed that Lauren and I share a family resemblance—Juliette never did. Doesn't that give you some indication of our marriage?'

She bit her lip. 'I'm good with faces.'

'Is that the real reason?' She flushed, and he went on quietly, 'With Juliette I knew there would be no loss of control, no passionate craving, no handing my heart over to someone who might treat it as carelessly as my father had treated my mother's. I chose the easy, safe, coward's path.'

Silence drummed between them until he said harshly, 'So it serves me right that when I saw you—a child of seventeen—two days before our wedding, I fell so hard and so fast I went into shock.'

Unable to speak, Paige sat stiffly, her eyes fixed on his hard face.

He finished, 'I don't believe in love at first sight, not

even now, but that's what happened to me. I married Juliette because I had made a vow to her and because I knew I would be safe with her. And if she hadn't died I would still be married to her.'

That flat, emphatic statement lifted Paige's heart, allowing her to hope. This man would keep a promise, no matter how much it cost him.

'I regret bitterly that she thought I was unfaithful,' he said bluntly. 'But, although she was pleased when I convinced her that it was untrue, she wouldn't have left me if it had been, Paige. She was content with what she had of me.' He paused. 'Just as I tried to convince myself that I was content with the path I'd chosen.'

She looked mutely at him, blinking at the blazing heat of his eyes. 'Then I saw you walk down the staircase from the strip club, and I knew that for six years I'd been lying to myself. The unruly passion I thought I'd killed had been hiding, and the moment I saw you with the child in your arms it burst out again—stronger for its repression, more violent than ever. And you felt it too—I saw it when you looked at me.'

'That's not love,' she said unsteadily.

'Perhaps not. But then I found that as well as being unbearably desirable you're compassionate, strong-willed, spirited and intelligent,' he said, his voice strained. 'And I want you in my life until I die. Is that love, Paige? Because if it is, I'm in love with you.'

Unable to believe what she'd heard, she stared at his dark, angular face in shock. 'In love?' she whispered.

'I don't know what else it can be.' He made an explicit Gallic gesture, his decisive hand slashing downwards. 'Passion is wonderful, and when we made love it was like nothing else I've ever experienced, but it is only part of what I feel for you.'

She jumped to her feet and advanced towards him, eyes glittering with tears. 'If you love me,' she demanded, 'why did you let me leave Arohanui? Why did you stay away for these past three dreadful months? You must have known how I felt about you, yet you, you—'

She grabbed his upper arms and shook him. It was like trying to move the Rock of Gibraltar. He didn't try to stop her, and when she made an exclamation of disgust at her own weakness he locked his fingers around her wrists, preventing her retreat.

In a low, caustic voice he said, 'I didn't want to feel this need. I dreaded being like my mother, weak-willed and dependent, enacting jealous rages, an abject slave to love. That's why I let you go, only to realise that without you there is nothing.'

He paused, a lethal gaze fixed intently on her face. 'And I hope you love me too. You were a virgin, yet you gave yourself to me—was that easy, ordinary lust?'

Colour flooded her skin, and just as rapidly faded. 'No,' she admitted on a long sigh. 'But, Marc—I'm not—I won't be a suitable wife for you.'

'I know,' he said, solemn-faced. 'In fact, you're outrageously unsuitable. I'll probably lose every cent of this money you find such a burden because I can't think of anything but you.'

She smiled, as he had meant her to, but it left her with twisted lips and she said uneasily, 'Your mother won't—'

'My mother wants me to be happy, and when she sees us together she'll know that I am.'

Paige stared up, read the complete conviction in his expression, and let herself hope. But before surrendering completely she said quietly, 'It's not that simple, Marc. You know that.'

'I know that together we can do anything we want to.'

His voice deepened. 'I know that my life is a desert without you. If you can't live in my world then I'll leave it and live with you, anywhere you want.'

Swift, hot tears ached behind her eyes. 'You'd get bored in a few months, and I wouldn't—I won't be happy unless you are.' She took a deep, ragged breath and fixed her eyes on his face. 'So if that means I have to learn how to behave in your world, I'll do it. I'm a quick learner, and if your mother will help—'

'She will,' he said, but he made no attempt to pull her where she longed to be, into his arms, against his heart.

He waited until she let down every barrier and took that first, terrifying step into the unknown.

'I do love you.' Her voice quivered, but she managed a smile in spite of the shimmer of tears. 'I've always loved you. And I want to make you so happy you won't ever regret it. If that's enough—'

'I want more than that.' His voice was slow and sure, vibrant with determination. 'I want to take such care of you that you never get ill again, or are unhappy again, or want—'

'Oh, Marc,' she whispered. 'You can't promise that.'

'I know.' He laughed softly and, finally yielding to his emotions, pulled her against him. 'But I'm going to try, my heart.'

At last convinced that this man would never use her or betray her, that she could trust him with her life and her love, she smiled crookedly at him. 'I will too,' she vowed. 'And I can see that we'll both be so over-protective we'll drive each other crazy.'

His arms closed around her as though she was something rare and preciously fragile. 'I can't wait. And I *can* promise that if you marry me we will always be together, that I'll always be there to support you, and that when you hybridise plants and call them after me and our children I'll be the proudest man in the world.'

She lifted a glowing face and kissed him, and after that there was no more talking, except in the deep, exquisite tenderness of love.

Later, lying in his arms on her bed, she traced a path through the pattern of fine hair across his chest and said sleepily, 'Now you can confess that you got Sherry her job.'

The wall of his chest lifted sharply beneath her finger. 'How did you know? She doesn't.'

'I guessed. It came very conveniently, and when I thought about it I couldn't really believe in people who'd overlook her past to hire her to look after their children—unless they knew more about her than that she was a stripper. Or unless they owed someone a favour.'

His eyes gleaming with lazy satisfaction, he pulled her exploring hand up to kiss the palm and then her wrist. Against the tumultuous pulse he admitted, 'They're friends. And they're delighted with her—so much so that now they owe me another favour for finding her for them.'

Paige looked at him with adoring delight. 'What made you do it for her?'

He paused, then shrugged, his skin sliding silkily, sensuously against hers. 'I liked her, and thought she deserved a better chance, but the main reason was that you were worried about her.'

'What about Juliette's legacy—the money?' When his mouth settled into a firm, inflexible line she leaned over and bit his earlobe. Into his ear she breathed, 'That came from you too, didn't it?'

'I can see I'm not going to have any secrets,' he complained wryly, easing her over onto her back. 'When did you work that out?'

'When you said you'd helped Sherry.' She lifted a hand and stroked his cheek, fingers tingling at the soft roughness of his beard beneath the sensitive tips.

He turned his head into her palm and said in a muffled voice, 'I couldn't bear the thought of you struggling on with no financial base to keep you safe. I had to make sure you were protected, that you had choices and options.'

Ten minutes before—only five minutes before!—Paige had believed that making love to Marc had more than sated her every desire. So she was surprised when that subtle heat began to smoulder again, this time reinforced by a deep, abiding gratitude to whatever fortunate fate had brought them together.

'I do love you,' she said, turning the simple words into a vow. 'I wish I hadn't thought you were such a horrible man.'

'You can make amends.' He slid his hand up to enclose one soft breast.

She laughed softly and kissed his shoulder. 'So I can,' she said wonderingly. 'I'm so happy! Everything seems newborn, as though loving you, knowing that you love me, has remade the world.'

'Good.' He traced the full contours of her mouth, his own softening into tenderness. 'I wondered if you could trust any man enough to love one. Your father left you, your boss harassed you, and your cousin died without making sure you and your mother had some sort of security. And I coldly and deliberately turned my back on a temptation I found unbearably enticing and married Juliette.'

'I fell in love with you on the telephone,' she confessed, 'at Arohanui when you rang every night. So I loved you before I knew you'd kept Lauren's secret, and that you were loyal to Juliette. I couldn't stop myself. It just happened.'

'I don't believe in fate. But then I didn't believe in love at first sight either! Perhaps we were meant to find each other, meant to love, meant to live a long and happy life together,' he said, and kissed her.

They were married on the island, a quiet simple ceremony with his mother and Lauren and Sherry and several of Marc's close friends. Afterwards, in the room she'd first slept in, Paige changed her ankle-length oyster-coloured silk gown for travelling clothes. They were spending their honeymoon on an island Marc owned in Tahiti, a small one in an isolated lagoon. Later they would fly to Paris, and then on to Venice.

Anticipation mingled in her with a tiny stab of foreboding. She looked down at her cream linen shirt and matching trousers and hoped she'd pass muster.

A brilliant blue flare from the ring Marc had given her comforted her. She turned it a little, admiring the colour. He'd suggested an emerald, but she'd decided on a Burmese sapphire the colour of his eyes. Glittering against the band of her wedding ring, it was a symbol of his commitment.

Not only was she utterly confident in Marc's love, confident enough to take on the world, but she had his mother's backing. At their first meeting Mrs Corbett had hugged her, and the last week had made it more than clear that Marc had been right—his mother only wanted his happiness, and was prepared to do whatever she could to forward it.

And she and Lauren were well on the way to becoming friends too. Marrying Marc had given her a family once

more. And there would be others—children, with his habit
of raising an ironic brow...

Smiling, she picked up her bag, and was making sure
she had everything she might need when a knock on the
door lifted her head. 'Come in,' she called.

But it was the housekeeper who came in, not Marc. She
looked a little worried, but she said, 'Mrs Corbett, I promised the—' she looked flustered, then recovered herself
'—the previous Mrs Corbett that I'd give you this if you
ever married Marc—Mr Corbett.'

'This' was an envelope with *Paige* written on it in
Juliette's elegant handwriting. A little chill ran down
Paige's spine.

'I hope it's all right,' the housekeeper said worriedly.
'She left me the two letters, you see—laughing a bit, because of course she didn't expect to die. One was to be
delivered when you came up to collect the bracelet, and
the other was if you married Marc.'

'Of course it's all right,' Paige said, hiding her momentary unease with a smile. 'Juliette was my friend.'

But the cold foreboding wormed its way into her as she
waited for the housekeeper to leave. Once the door had
closed behind Mrs Oliver, Paige slowly opened the envelope, sitting on the edge of the bed to read the note inside.

Dearest Paige,
*If you're reading this then I'll have been dead for at
least two years and you'll have married Marc. I want
you to know that you have my blessing.*
  *I feel silly writing this, but I need to. Not long ago I
had a dream. I was lying in a swan boat with flowers
all around me, lovely carnations and roses and long
branches of mock orange in full white flower. Although*

*it was strange, I was happy and excited, because I knew
I was going somewhere wonderful, and that once I got
there I'd meet someone wonderful. Then you and Marc
walked out of the mist and stood looking down at me.
You were crying, and Marc's face was all stony, the
way it goes when he doesn't want anyone to know what
he's thinking, yet you were linked in a shining glow, a
kind of radiance. I tried to tell you both that I was
happy, not to worry about me, not to grieve, but I
couldn't talk or move.*

Paige's heart clenched in her breast. She put the sheets
of paper down on the bed, but picked them up almost
immediately with trembling hands and read the rest.

*I knew that this was the way things were meant to be.
It was a lovely sureness, a certainty, and it stayed with
me when I woke up. Of course it was just a dream, but
in case it wasn't, dearest Paige, sister of my heart, then
I know that one day you'll be reading this and that you
and Marc will make each other very happy.*

*It's why I left you my bracelet on such strange con-
ditions. I wanted you to stay on the island so that you
and Marc would get to know each other, but it had to
be long enough after my death for neither of you to be
constrained by sorrow. Two years, I decided, was a
good period.*

She'd signed it *My love to you both*, and under the signature she'd added:

*By the way, Marc told me he has never had an affair
with his English executive, and I believe him. There is*

a connection there, but it is not sexual or romantic.
Dearest Paige, be very happy.

Paige was still sitting on the bed, her eyes drowned in tears, when Marc came in.

'What is it?' he demanded, quick anger abrading his voice.

Wordlessly she held the letter out to him.

He frowned, but took it and read it. Then he pulled her up into his arms and said into her hair, 'I didn't know— she never told me.'

Shivering, Paige leaned gratefully against him, absorbing his warm strength, the unfailing support she knew would be hers always. 'It's—uncanny. And not like Juliette—she was so pragmatic.' She drew in a shaking breath. 'I hope—I hope that after the accident she woke up in her golden swan boat, surrounded with her favourite flowers and drenched in their perfume.'

He said soberly, 'The accident investigators told me she'd have had one moment of fear, perhaps, and then oblivion. She didn't suffer, my dearest heart. And if this dream gave her some sort of comfort, I'm glad. As glad as I am that she tried to set us up together. Some unconscious part of her must have recognised the—the affinity between us.'

Paige nodded into his shoulder.

He went on, 'After she died I told myself I'd wait the two years she'd stipulated and then hand her keepsake over to you and that would be an end to this inconvenient obsession. But the moment I saw you again I knew I'd lied. It was never going to end, and it wasn't obsession. It was love. Not that I was ready to admit that to myself—I was too afraid.'

Startled, Paige looked up. 'Afraid? You?'

'You still don't know how much you mean to me,' he told her, smoothing a strand of bright hair back from her temple. He held her away from him and looked into her face, his own at last naked and open to her, not trying to hide the deep, powerful emotions she saw there.

Blue fire leaping in his eyes, he said thickly, 'If I were a poet I could find new ways to tell you what I feel. But I can only say what so many men have said before, that I love you. I'll spend the rest of my life trying to convince you that those three words contain everything important to me.'

Paige met his brilliant gaze with courage and a happiness that turned her eyes to pure shimmering gold. 'And I love you,' she said very softly. 'With all my heart, all that I am. I always will.'

He laughed, the deep, triumphant laugh of a lover, and dropped a swift kiss on her nose. 'Then let's go. We've got a whole, glorious, magnificent lifetime together to discover all the facets of our love. I can't wait to start.'

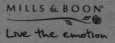

Modern Romance™
...seduction and
passion guaranteed

Tender Romance™
...love affairs that
last a lifetime

Medical Romance™
...medical drama
on the pulse

Historical Romance™
...rich, vivid and
passionate

Sensual Romance™
...sassy, sexy and
seductive

Blaze Romance™
...the temperature's
rising

27 new titles every month.

Live the emotion

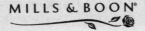

MILLS & BOON®

MB3

FREE!

4 Books
and a surprise gift!

We would like to take this opportunity to thank you for reading this Mills & Boon® book by offering you the chance to take FOUR more specially selected titles from the Modern Romance™ series absolutely FREE! We're also making this offer to introduce you to the benefits of the Reader Service™ —

    ★ FREE home delivery
    ★ FREE gifts and competitions
    ★ FREE monthly Newsletter
    ★ Books available before they're in the shops
    ★ Exclusive Reader Service discount

Accepting these FREE books and gift places you under no obligation to buy; you may cancel at any time, even after receiving your free shipment. Simply complete your details below and return the entire page to the address below. **You don't even need a stamp!**

YES! Please send me 4 free Modern Romance books and a surprise gift. I understand that unless you hear from me, I will receive 6 superb new titles every month for just £2.60 each, postage and packing free. I am under no obligation to purchase any books and may cancel my subscription at any time. The free books and gift will be mine to keep in any case.

P3ZEF

Ms/Mrs/Miss/Mr ....Initials..
                                                                           BLOCK CAPITALS PLEASE

Surname ....

Address ....

....

....Postcode ....

Send this whole page to:
UK: The Reader Service, FREEPOST CN81, Croydon, CR9 3WZ
EIRE: The Reader Service, PO Box 4546, Kilcock, County Kildare (stamp required)